Her freedom lay within easy reach

Yet Anstey hesitated. The young Jacobites, anxious that she grasp this opportunity to flee with them back to the safety of Scotland, pleaded with her to take action.

But still Anstey stood, her eyes riveted on the fallen English captain, the man who'd held her prisoner. Suddenly she knew what she must do.

Ordering her would-be rescuers to leave without her, she knelt and tended the wounded man, heedless of the fact that to stay with him might cost her her life!

COME WITH US
ON A ROMANTIC JOURNEY
TO THE PAST...

As publishers of **Masquerade** historical romances, we want to take you to the fascinating world of romance and intrigue in times gone by.

Masquerade romances will sweep you back to a distant day filled with lavish balls and masked ladies, wicked conspiracies and vicious highwaymen–a world filled with intrigue and danger...but most of all with love.

We know you will treasure these very special love stories, for each is a reading experience you won't forget. Every month two new, never-before-in-paperback volumes are published. You'll find them wherever paperback books are sold.

Bon Voyage

Sincerely,

Masquerade

The Rebel and the Redcoat

JAN CONSTANT

A MASQUERADE FROM

W🌐RLDWIDE

TORONTO · LONDON · NEW YORK

Masquerade edition published August 1980
ISBN 0-373-30047-6

Originally published in 1980
by Mills & Boon Limited

Printed in Canada

CHAPTER
ONE

THE wind from the sea snatched at the girl's skirt and stirred the soft tendrils of dark blonde hair that escaped from the plaited coronet she wore as she paused in the doorway of the tower, lifting her face into the chill air with the enjoyment of one who had not felt fresh air for some time. Heedless of her guard's impatience, she looked about as she folded a tartan shawl around her shoulders, watching a seagull as it hung in the breeze and following it with her eyes as it plunged away with a raucous cry.

The man touched her arm and she followed him reluctantly, her footsteps lingering as she crossed the castle courtyard. Looking over the stone wall, she could see the waters of the loch below and the white sand of the shallow shore, while beyond a group of tiny houses clustered about the far end of the stone causeway that joined the island of Cushlan Keep to the mainland.

"Sir Robert is waiting," said the man at her elbow.

Anstey Frazer turned her shoulder and gazed over the blue sea that reflected the summer sky, her dark eyes intent as if she were memorizing the scene before her.

"The English Redcoat is with him," the man went on.

"I know, for I saw the soldiers arrive." She smiled coolly at the man. "But I fail to see why that should make me hurry when this is the first time I've seen the outside of your tower for more than a week."

"Indeed, Mistress, and I ken fine your feeling, but the Chief'll no' be in a good mood if you keep him waiting – especially with the Redcoat to see him so disrespectfully treated."

"Your master's moods have little importance for me," Anstey told him loftily, but at length she turned and followed the clansman into the tall crenellated keep, her smallness emphasised by the pair of massive wooden doors.

The man behind the table rose at her entrance, and came forward with hand outstretched and all the signs of a welcoming host.

"Good evening, Mistress Anstey," he said. "Will you take a glass of wine?"

"Not with you, Sir Robert," Anstey replied, eyeing him coldly. "I've tasted your hospitality in your prison tower for the last week and that's enough."

"You knew you could have spent the time as a guest in the castle – I've even asked you to dine with me."

"I'll have no dealings with a traitor!"

"Anstey!" Sir Robert glanced over his shoulder at the silent figure in the window embrasure, who had turned and was regarding the scene with obvious interest, his tall form and broad shoulders silhouetted against the light.

"If you're afraid of what your English friend will learn, I'll tell him it's not your politics I question, but your loyalty to old friends. My father saved your life as a child, and for that he was given a piece of Mackenzie

land, which you've always coveted and now see a way
of recovering."

"The land belongs to the family – my father had no
right to give it to a stranger. I could have accepted gold
or money, but not my inheritance."

"So now, with my father attainted for following the
Stuart Prince, my brother a fugitive and myself
accused of murder, you see a way of seizing it?"

"If you'd married me, Anstey, as I asked, this
would never have happened." He spoke quickly and
sincerely, forgetting the silent stranger behind him.

Anstey regarded him, her lip curling contemptuously. "You thought you'd get Glentyre through me,"
she told him scornfully. "Did you really think I'd
marry you, when your wife had been my friend and I'd
seen how you treated her – and even your children
afraid of you? I'd too much care for my own wellbeing
to even consider it, Robert Mackenzie!"

Sir Robert checked a sudden movement towards
her, and recalling the watching soldier forced a laugh
to his lips, the angry colour high in his cheeks.

"See what a spirit our Highland lasses have?" he
asked jocularly. "I don't envy you your task of carrying her to London. Take my advice and don't believe a
word she says."

The soldier gazed at Anstey, noting the air of
defiance she wore like a cloak, his eyes travelling over
her neat Highland costume of blue velvet bodice and
short, full skirt of tartan.

"Pray introduce us," he said quietly.

"Captain James Ward – Mistress Frazer," Sir
Robert supplied curtly.

The English soldier bowed his powdered head, his

red coat and white breeches incongruous to Anstey's eyes, used to the kilt or tartan trews. She acknowledged the introduction with the briefest of nods, and with chin high, waited for him to speak.

"I have been sent to escort you to London where you will stand trial for murder of one of the King's officers."

He thought she grew pale, but her voice when she spoke was firm and clear.

"I suppose that you feel an English jury would be more likely to convict."

He raised his eyebrows. "Is there some doubt of your guilt?"

"None whatsoever – I confessed at once."

Captain Ward looked to the Scotsman for confirmation.

"Just so – besides, there can be no doubt at all. She was found by the soldiers with the pistol in her hand and the body of the officer at her feet."

The soldier looked at her with distaste. "Spirit indeed," he observed coldly. "Thank God our English women are more civilised."

"Have your English women had to defend their lives against a cruel invader?" Anstey asked hotly. "Better give your thanks that they haven't had to face the barbarities shown after Culloden. None of our leaders have earned the title of 'Butcher' as your fat duke has."

"War has a way of making barbarians of us all, Miss Frazer, as you have found out –"

"War, Captain Ward, had very little to do with it. Your soldiers arrived to turn me from my house due to the machinations of Sir Robert."

"Your father is a Jacobite, he was out with the Pretender and has since fled to France. It was my duty –" put in Sir Robert.

"Duty!" exploded Anstey. "You wouldn't know what duty was. It was sheer greed – you wanted Glentyre and saw the chance of taking it, so you informed your English cronies and even sent men to guide them here. I despise you, Robert Mackenzie, you are less than half the man your father was. I hope you think at night how he must be turning in his grave to know of the thanks you gave to the man who saved your life . . . And now I would go back to my cell."

"I've said you'll dine with us," Sir Robert said, his face tight with anger.

"I'll not break bread with you."

"Nevertheless you'll sit at my board, if I have to tie you there."

Anstey Frazer laughed shortly. "So that you can tell the tale to your credit of how you offered me food the night before I was taken to England? Sir Robert, the folk hereabouts know you better than that. Your greed and cruelty are common knowledge."

" 'Fore God I pray they hang you," he said through his clenched teeth.

"Whatever happens to me, I'm certain that you will roast in Hell."

For a moment Captain Ward was certain that the Scotsman would strike her, but, aware of the witness, Sir Robert regained control of himself and shouted for the table to be spread.

Anxious servants ran in carrying dishes of vegetables and a plate of boiled mutton. Sir Robert seated himself at the head of the table and indicated that his guests should take either side. Captain Ward held the chair for Anstey, and reading the expression in the Scotman's eyes which said only too plainly that he would enjoy carrying out his threat, she reluctantly took the seat, but resolutely refused all food and drink.

Captain Ward sighed over his plate, having discovered that invariably the meat was badly prepared and cooked, either tough or underdone, and usually accompanied by soggy, overcooked cabbage.

"I'm afraid that Captain Ward does not approve of your cook, Sir Robert," said Anstey wickedly, having recognised the fleeting expression of distaste that had passed over the soldier's face.

Ignoring her jibe, James Ward turned to his host and asked him some questions on Highland economy, a matter dear to Sir Robert's heart, and for a while Anstey was left to herself. When she thought herself unobserved the defiance left her expression, leaving her eyes shadowed with fear and her mouth vulnerable as she toyed with her glass, twisting the long stem between her fingers as she stared into the clear bowl.

Pipes were lit and she lifted her head at the first smell of tobacco. "Let me go now," she said, a hint of a plea in her voice.

Sir Robert blew smoke in her direction. "I'm sure you can ask better than that," he said.

"Let me go, Sir Robert," she repeated wearily.

For a moment their eyes held across the littered table, then Robert Mackenzie made an impatient gesture.

"Go, then, and be damned to you – I hope never to see you again."

Anstey looked at him steadily, nodded slightly and

rising, went to the door. Sir Robert hunched an indifferent shoulder, giving his attention to refilling his glass, but the soldier crossed the room and held the door for her.

"We set out early," he warned, and put her into the care of a waiting guard before closing the door and returning to his host.

Anstey followed the broad back of Sir Robert's retainer, so deep in thought that she scarcely raised her head as she crossed the courtyard and held her skirt down automatically as the wind lifted it about her ankles.

The Redcoat officer had seemed quiet and gentlemanly in his manners, she thought, but there had been a certain coldness at the back of his eyes when he looked at her, that caused her unease. She sensed a dislike which was more personal than was to be expected in a soldier merely performing a duty, however distasteful. Finding no satisfactory explanation, she dismissed the matter from her mind and gave her attention to her plans for the morrow; knowing the countryside as she did, she felt sure that she could give Captain Ward some surprises and fell to planning her actions.

Anstey had made her scanty toilet and eaten the water and porridge supplied for her breakfast, when the door to her cell was opened and the tall form of Captain Ward appeared, filling the small doorway.

"Pray put these on," he said, holding out a bundle of clothing.

Puzzled, Anstey took them, shaking out the folded garments. "But these are breeks!" she gasped.

"I can imagine that your sensibility must be shocked by such a request, but I do assure you that I consider it necessary," he told her formally.

"I'll not wear men's clothes," Anstey stated, thrusting the green woollen suit from her. "You must be mad to ask such a thing. Even King George would not expect a lady to display herself in such a manner. You've seen too many plays, Captain, where I hear actresses are only too pleased to show off their charms. Even Sir Robert would—"

"Sir Robert, I may say, was in favour of it when I told him my plans," said the soldier, his eyes glinting as he looked down at her wrathful face.

She was brought up short by his reply and then gave a short laugh. "Because he fears some of my people might try to effect a rescue and they would be less likely to recognize me in such a disguise!" she cried scornfully.

"I believe he had something like that in mind, but that is not wholly the reason in my case. My troopers would have little difficulty in dealing with an un-armed rabble. The journey is long and difficult and I should say quite impossible riding side-saddle and encumbered by heavy voluminous skirts. For your own safety, I must insist that you wear breeches."

Anstey eyed him with clear dislike. "You can take that air of complacency off your face," she told him roundly, "for I'm not a female to be reasoned with. I've no intention of showing my legs in your suit, and that's an end of it."

"Then, Miss Frazer," the Captain said quietly, "you'll show a good deal more, for if you don't put them on yourself, I'll call my troopers to act as lady's maids and dress you to my liking."

Anstey's gaze widened and her shocked eyes flew to his face, her expression indicative of the outrage she felt. "You would not dare!" she gasped.

Amusement gleamed momentarily in the Redcoat's eyes. "Take my advice and don't rely on that," he drawled.

A few seconds longer she held his gaze, before her defence crumbled under his indomitable air.

"Very well," she whispered, "but go away."

"You may have ten minutes," he announced curtly and left.

Once alone, mindful of the time-limit imposed, Anstey scrambled into the unfamiliar clothes, pausing as she suddenly recognized them as belonging to her younger brother. Stroking the wool of the jacket, she wondered if he had managed to effect his escape to France; then, recalling the passing of the minutes, she dragged on the waistcoat, her fingers fumbling with the long line of buttons. She was still struggling with the lawn cravat when, after the briefest of knocks, the soldier returned.

His eyes travelled over her without expression and she flushed and shifted her weight from foot to foot under his scrutiny. Silently he reached forward and finished tying the cravat around her neck, then, taking her by the shoulders, turned her about.

"We'll have to do something about your hair," he said as he removed the pins from the coronet she wore high on her head, and her hair spilled on to her shoulders.

For a moment his fingers were cool on the nape of

her neck as he gathered the loose, dark blonde tresses together and Anstey shivered under his impersonal touch.

"I will do it," she said, not liking the intimacy, and moving pointedly away. The grasp on her hair was retained and she was brought up short by his grip. Hearing an odd sawing sound, she twisted to see what he was doing and saw to her dismay a tumble of hair fall to the ground.

"It will grow again," he said heartlessly, tying a black ribbon about what was left of her hair and standing back to examine her. "You make quite a passable young man," he commented dryly.

More upset by the loss of her hair than she wished him to know, Anstey stared stonily back, determined to keep the tears from her eyes as Captain Ward took her arm and led her from the tiny room.

The clear early morning light dazzled her momentarily as they arrived in the courtyard, and at first she could only see her escort as dim, formless figures, but her vision cleared quickly and she was able to make out several horses and men in bright uniforms waiting nearby. As she emerged all eyes were turned on her and she read both curiosity and anger in their hostile glances.

A small black horse was led towards her, and the Captain commented that he hoped she could ride astride.

"She'll have learnt by the time we reach London," observed his sergeant, and Anstey looked quickly at the older man, reading in his expression the same hostility that was emitted from the troopers.

"Of course she can – our women ride astride on all

but the most formal occasions," said a voice from the top of the steps to the keep, and they all turned to look at its owner.

"Come to wish me Godspeed?" Anstey asked as the Sergeant cupped his hands for her booted foot and she was thrown into the saddle.

"I've a mind to make sure the captain knows how to treat you," Sir Robert told her, descending the stone steps. "Take my advice, Captain Ward, and tie her in the saddle – if you have no irons to fasten her wrists."

The officer looked faintly surprised. "I'm sure there is no need for such matters."

"I've known Anstey Frazer all her life and while you might think her meek and mild, I know she's planning her escape. She's slippery as an eel and as wily as a fox, so have a care and take heed of my warning."

"Tut, Sir Robert – the soldiers will think you lack the manners of a gentleman."

"Oh, I'm a fine gentleman. Today, for instance, I'm going hunting just like my English fellows."

Anstey's eyes narrowed as she looked down at him from the back of her mount. "Hunting – that's not one of your hobbies that I know about."

"Hunting Jacobites is better sport than chasing a fox or deer. Your brother has been missing for more than a week. I intend to run him to earth today."

Anstey caught her breath, but her voice was steady when she replied. "You'll not find him," she said with conviction.

"You think not? Who knows, perhaps I'll find your sister instead, and maybe she'll be more amenable to my proposals than yourself."

The girl was so pale that James Ward thought she

was about to faint and instinctively stepped nearer.

"You wouldn't," she whispered, "not even you, Robert Mackenzie, would do such a thing."

The Scotsman laughed triumphantly. "I would, Mistress Anstey, and fine you know it, so take that thought away with you. When you mount the scaffold she and I may even then be wed."

Captain Ward felt there was much here he did not understand. "This sister?" he asked. "What of her?"

"She's an idiot," Sir Robert told him briefly, not taking his eyes from the girl.

The Englishman was shocked. "And you'd marry her?"

"Her body's fine and healthy – she'll bear many a bairn." Sir Robert eyed Anstey reflectively. "And she's prettier than this one. Flaxen-haired and beautiful, with the face of an angel."

Captain Ward was not interesed in his lyrical description. "How long's she been missing?" he demanded, watching the slight figure in green intently.

"Since the day of the murder," Sir Robert supplied and taking his meaning went on impatiently, "She's an idiot, man, and wouldn't have enough sense to shoot. No – you can be sure that her sister got her out of the way in case the soldiery took a fancy to her. She's a beauty, as I've told you." The soldier seemed unconvinced, but Sir Robert was so confident and persuasive that he allowed himself to accept the obvious culprit presented to him and, giving the order to mount, took a curt leave of his host and led the way across the stone causeway to the mainland.

At first the troopers rode close to her, but as Anstey

allowed the dejection she felt to show in the dispirited droop to her shoulders, their tension relaxed and they began to straggle. By the time they had left the castle a mile behind them they had accepted that she presented no danger and were so strung out on the rough road that when Anstey and the first of the escort rode under a clump of spindly trees, she was able to reach up, seize a low overhanging branch and by pulling hard on it and letting it go suddenly, spring it back in the riders' faces. Before they had recovered their wits she had slipped off her horse and, slapping its rump, sent it careering along the track while she ran behind a rock and into a narrow fissure, hidden from view but familiar from her many visits to the croft to which it led.

Taking to her heels with the speed of desperation, she scrambled down the narrow path between high sides of overhanging rock until they opened out suddenly into a bay with the small croft house nestling against the circling cliffs. Mindful of the foolhardiness of her action, Anstey plunged on, not thinking of her own danger or that of her friends, only aware that she must have news of her brother before she left Scotland; perhaps for ever.

At the sound of her approach the clumsy door was opened and she slipped into the interior, blackened by generations of peat smoke. "Redcoats are after me, Catlin," she said breathlessly to the small child regarding her. "If they come here, can you say you've seen no one?"

With her finger in her mouth the girl nodded, and at that moment they heard the sounds of approaching footsteps.

"Dear God, I shouldn't have come," murmured Anstey, appalled by the realisation of what she had done, "but I had to know about my brother – is he away?" Before the little girl could reply someone beat a tattoo upon the door, making the occupants stare at each other in dismay and without a word Catlin opened the door a narrow crack and slipped through.

"Have you seen anyone? A woman – a young man in a green suit?"

There was silence and Anstey could imagine Catlin shaking her head. Muttered oaths and shouted orders and the sound of falling shingle told her that the neighbouring cliffs were being searched, and then a frightened wail from the little girl made her catch her breath and start towards the door.

"Come out, Miss Frazer, or it will be the worse for the child," called Captain Ward, his voice so grim and uncompromising that Anstey knew he meant his threat and, dragging the door open, left her refuge.

The English soldier gripped Catlin's arm, the child's frightened eyes fixed on the huge pistol in his other hand.

"Let her go!" Anstey cried sharply, hurrying forward and at once the girl was set free and the Captain calmly replacing the weapon in his belt.

"It wasn't even cocked!" cried the Scots girl upon sudden realisation.

"We don't make war on children," she was told loftily.

"But – you do cheat."

He shrugged indifferently as she bent over the girl who had flown into her arms. Anstey hugged her tightly and murmured soothingly against her hair while she suddenly realised to her surprise that the child was taking the opportunity to whisper to her.

"Your brother's no' away just yet," came the slight voice. "My father will look after him – but he's still out on the mountain."

For answer Anstey hugged her closer and dropped a swift kiss on the smooth cheek.

"Come, Miss Frazer, we've lost enough time," said the Captain, growing impatient.

As though to say farewell the child came closer, leaning against Anstey's leg for a moment and the confiding gesture hid the slight movement and pressure as something was slipped into her riding-boot.

A meaning glance was exchanged before the child slid silently away and ran back to the croft on bare feet.

Anstey was led back to the head of the gorge and pushed impatiently into her saddle. James Ward, who had intercepted the gaze between them, mounted his own horse and rode to face her, taking her reins in his hand.

"You realize the danger you put that child in?" he demanded, his voice harsh. "Had we been the ogres you say we are, she could have been dead and her home a burnt shell by now."

Anstey smiled sweetly. "But, Captain, I've been in your company and that of your excellent troopers long enough to realize that you are all models of virtue and kindness."

His mouth tightened ominously and Anstey was intrigued to see that for the first time she had managed to disturb the tight control he kept on his emotions.

"Indeed, I am only puzzled as to how these wild

stories of outrage and atrocities arose. With the examples before me I'd have supposed King George's men more likely to chuck children's chins and dangle babies upon their knees, than kill wounded men and burn helpless women in their houses."

"Enough," he said, abruptly. "Your own example is hardly to be lauded."

For the moment she had forgotten to what he alluded and stared at him blankly, while he, reading her puzzled expression, snorted in derision.

"Don't try that innocent expression with me, Miss Frazer," he said. "I am well aware that you found yourself able to kill a man in cold blood."

"What do you know – ?" she began hotly, caught unawares, only to break off abruptly, biting her lip.

"I know enough having read the sworn affidavits of Leo Smythe's sergeant and troopers. That he entered Glentyre alone in order not to alarm you unduly, and that hearing a shot sometime later, they ran in to find you standing over his lifeless body with a spent pistol in your hand." He regarded her coldly, his eyes like ice and his expression contemptuous. "Don't attempt the excuse that he molested you, for not only was your dress quite undisturbed, but I've known Captain Smythe since our schooldays and am well aware that such an action would be totally beyond him."

"Strange things happen, Captain Ward," she remarked quietly, her voice trembling slightly.

"He had recently lost his wife in childbed – I assure you that he would have had not the slightest interest in any female."

"You were not there," she burst out.

"I refuse to listen further to your wild and groundless accusations. Indeed I feel it only fair to warn you against pursuing them. Captain Smythe was a very popular officer and well liked by my men."

Anstey remembered the open hostility she had seen on the troopers' faces that morning and shivered a little, her shoulders shaking under the green jacket.

Captain Ward watched her, his face hard. "I have allowed you more leniency than I should," he remarked. "It would obviously be wise to restrain your liberty and with that in mind I have a pair of hand-irons among the baggage. However," he paused, having been satisfied to see the flicker of horror that had passed over her face, "as they would be uncomfortable and the road is difficult, I would be prepared to accept your word of honour not to make a further attempt to escape."

Anstey avoided his eyes, gazing past him and out to sea, watching the purple islands silhouetted against the horizon before her eyes returned reluctantly to her near surroundings. "You have it," she told him gravely, and felt a surge of excitement as she gave the promise she had no intention of keeping.

CHAPTER
TWO

THE midday meal was a hasty affair, eaten by the road beside a small stream that fed its brown peaty water from a spring high up on the nearby cliff. Anstey took her bread and cheese down to the hollow it had worn for itself and finding a sheltered spot settled herself against a boulder and found, once seated, that she was out of sight of the English soldiers. Their voices faded to a hum behind her and she found that by dint of imagination she could almost believe that the events of the last two weeks had not happened and that she and her brother Jamie were exploring the familiar countryside around Glentyre.

The thought of her brother brought to her mind the catastrophic events that had happened when the Redcoats arrived at her home and involuntarily she suppressed a groan and hid her head in her hands, wondering if she would ever see her family or Glentyre again.

Suddenly the food was tasteless and she tossed it to a circling seagull before bending forward to scoop up some water in the palm of her hand and savour the familiar taste of the peat it carried. A sound behind her made her stiffen and, still on her knees, she turned her head; Captain Ward was watching her, one foot on a rock, his elbow on his raised knee, and she wondered how long he had been there. By the stillness of his position she judged that he had not arrived recently and scrambled to her feet, hastily flicking away the signs of her recent tears.

"I must ask you not to go out of sight," he said.

"We all need privacy at times, sir," she answered, "but now I know how silent of foot you are, I shall take care that all know my intentions and so none can play the part of a spy."

He flushed a little at the insinuation and straightened abruptly. "Pray have the goodness to rejoin my troop," he commanded stiffly, his eyes on a point above her head.

Anstey considered him, her head on one side. "I notice that you have brought none of your men with you," she commented, deliberately provoking. "Does that mean that you are one of these officers we hear about? Would you contrive to let me escape – if I paid you enough?"

She moistened her lips slowly and smiled in what she hoped was an enticing manner, aware that her action was somewhat marred by the masculine garments she was wearing. However recalling that most men found actresses who besported themselves upon the stage in boys' parts attractive, she struck a pose and puffed out her chest.

Captain Ward's reaction was unexpected. Striding forward so quickly that she had no time to step back, he seized both her arms above the elbow and shook her.

"Have a care, madam, that you don't try your tricks on my troopers," he told her harshly, his face close to hers. "Doubtless they would accept your invitation, with results which you might not intend. As for myself, you may as well understand that even had I not held my honour dear, nothing would induce me to help you escape or avoid the fate which you so rightly deserve. Leo Smythe was a good officer and a dear friend, remember that, Miss Frazer; and the fact that even were it not my duty as a soldier of the King, I would still not rest until you are hanged!"

He released her with the words, and suddenly pale Anstey stepped back, her eyes dark with fear and anticipation. Unable to hide her trembling, she turned and stumbling a little, hurried back to the road.

Feeling sick with fear she hunched in the saddle, heedless of her surroundings of majestic mountains and sparkling burns, and knew that her one hope lay in escaping. She viewed Captain Ward's grimness of purpose with something approaching horror, and had already begun to suspect that he was totally ruthless in that which he considered his duty.

Looking at his straight back as he rode at the head of his men, she could not suppress a shiver, and biting her lips looked hastily away and encountered the gaze of a young trooper riding nearby. Something in his expression encouraged her, and hungry for some sign of friendship, she smiled tentatively.

An engaging grin spread across his sunburned face and she realized that he was even younger than she had supposed; only a few years older than Jamie. The soldier nodded slightly before returning to the wooden pose expected of him and her mood of despair lightened beyond all reason. Anstey rode on, the sun suddenly warm on her back. Looking about, she found her surroundings, now that she was leaving them, more beautiful than she ever remembered.

Taking advantage of the long Highland daylight, they rode on into the evening, coming at last upon a small settlement where the Captain intended to spend the night. Anstey was too tired to do more than peck at the meal provided and fell asleep in the lodgings arranged for her, hoping as she curled up in the cramped bed, built like a cupboard into the wall, that she would not provide a meal for the unwelcome bedfellows which she suspected throve among the blankets.

The day was not far advanced when they set off the next morning. The dew was wet underfoot and the horses' hooves sent up showers of spray at every step. Anstey felt her spirits rise unaccountably as she saw the mountain path which they must take, winding upwards ahead between buttresses of rock and wooded slopes. Here, she knew, was her chance of escape. Surreptitiously watching the soldiers, she saw their unease in the unfamiliar surroundings, as they loosened the weapons in their sheaths and glanced cautiously around, as though expecting hordes of fierce clansmen to dash out of hiding at any moment.

The order for single file was given and her heart rose, only to sink as Captain Ward's eye fell on her and he ordered a Trooper Gray to take her rein. To her scarcely concealed elation, the soldier who rode forward was the boy who had shown friendliness the day before.

"I'm glad it was you," she confided in a whisper.

"Are you, miss?" He seemed pleased.

"All the others seem such ogres, I vow I'm afraid of them."

His gaze travelled over his companions, seeing them with Anstey's eyes. "Well, I suppose they might," he concluded, having taken in their stained red uniforms and powdered hair strained back under tall black caps, "but they're good fellows really."

"None smiled at me, save you. Tell me your name, Trooper Gray."

"It's Johnnie, miss –"

He broke off abruptly as the sergeant rode up, his shrewd blue eyes going from one to the other.

"No fraternising, Trooper," he said. "Remember, the prisoner has a way with Redcoats, that's why we're taking her to London."

Dropping back when he was certain his words had sunk in, he rode behind them, but Anstey was conscious of his watchful eyes boring into her back and dared not do more than cast a fleeting glance in the direction of her young companion. She saw that he was riding with his eyes straight ahead, a bright flush on his cheeks, and thought despairingly that his tentative friendship had been lost before it had begun. But a little later she was surprised to hear a hoarse whisper.

"I know as how you didn't do it – and if you did, it was to save your honour," Johnnie Gray assured her, and she sent him a grateful glance.

"No talking in the ranks," shouted the sergeant from behind, and they quickly turned their eyes ahead and rode on in silence, both aware of an affinity between them.

That midday Johnnie Gray brought Anstey's bread and cheese to her and she looked up in surprise as he sat down beside her.

"I thought the sergeant didn't like 'fraternising'."

He grinned. "He doesn't, miss, but the Captain says it's good for me to learn to do my duty. He says I must regard you as a prisoner and forget that you are a female and attractive."

"Did he say that?" asked Anstey. "About me being attractive?"

"Well, he *did* say a 'fancy piece', but that's soldiers' talk for the same thing."

Catching his anxious eye, Anstey felt her mouth twitch and suddenly they were laughing together, trying to suppress their mirth in case it was noticed by the others.

"I'm glad you're here, Johnnie Gray," she told him, "I need a friend."

He sobered at her words and studied her anxiously, his brow furrowed. "You shouldn't be here, miss," he said slowly. "The others do say as how when you get to London, you'll be –" He swallowed the next word and looked away.

"Hanged," supplied Anstey, her voice calm. "Yes, I know!" She watched the effect on the boy.

"It's not right," he said miserably. "If only I could help."

Anstey studied him thoughtfully. "If I could get away," she suggested carefully, "I could hide in the mountains and they'd never find me. I'd only need a moment – if somebody could bar the way for a second, that's all I need." She moved closer, and holding his eyes with hers, touched her neck. "I don't want to die, Johnnie," she said, and allowed the fear she felt to show in her voice.

"I can't do it, miss," he cried, aghast.

"Please," she whispered desperately. "*Please*."

The boy scrambled to his feet, scattering crumbs from his lap in his haste, and quickly walked away, leaving her to follow more slowly. Avoiding his eyes as he helped her to mount, she supposed him to have refused her request and felt depression settle heavily about her.

Later that afternoon she saw ahead the perfect place for her escape; ahead the road narrowed into a gorge while an even narrower track led between a fissure in the rock walls. Wild hope surged through her.

"Johnnie," she breathed, "here's the place – help me."

Waiting until she was level with the fissure which no one else seemed to have noticed, she suddenly spun her mount on his hind legs and plunged off the road, urging him along the steep, rocky path at a gallop, while behind her came shouts and the sound of altercation, and flinging a glance backwards she saw Johnnie barring the way.

Her heart beating wildly with excitement, Anstey clapped her heels into the horse's sides and crouching low over his neck, used all her skill as a rider to draw every possible ounce of speed out of him. Suddenly she was out of the confining sides of the fissure and had emerged upon a bare mountainside, its undulating slopes sweeping upwards without a scrap of cover upon them.

A clatter of hooves and falling stones behind made her glance over her shoulder in time to see Captain Ward emerge from the fissure, his mount rearing and plunging before being turned in her direction. Anstey was uncertain whether she would have stopped at the soldier's shout or not, but her horse was in his stride by now and carried away by excitement, seized his head and hurtled away across the slope towards the distant mountain top.

Needing all her skill to stay in the saddle, Anstey crouched low and prayed that he would not trip or put his hoof in a rabbit-hole. The chase was short; before they had travelled more than a few hundred yards at high speed, she was aware of a horse's outstretched head and neck at her elbow, and then a strong, brown hand reached out to seize her bridle in an iron grip. Slowly but inevitably they came to a sweating, breathless halt, and she raised a hand to put back her hair that had broken loose from its confining ribbon in her wild flight.

The rage in his cold grey eyes took her aback; she had expected anger, but was unprepared for the look of near-loathing which he directed at her, his mouth a tight line, his cheeks knotted with tension. Without a word, he dragged the horse's head round and set off towards the fissure they had so lately left, stopping only to snatch up and toss to her the tricorne hat that she had lost during the chase.

Anstey felt her heart beat a mad tattoo against her ribs as they hurried back to the road and found Captain Ward's ominous silence even more disturbing than a noisy anger would have been.

Rejoining the waiting troop, her eyes sought Johnnie Gray, finding him at last, a miserable dejected figure, sitting his horse with hanging head amidst the other soldiers. The troopers regarded her with blank, hostile eyes and she knew that they blamed her for the young Redcoat's action.

Without more ado the gorge was left behind and

they rode on until, coming upon a level place with a good view of the surrounding countryside, they stopped and dismounted, the soldiers seeming to know what to do and each going about his task in a grim silence.

Anstey watched, sensing that something unpleasant was about to take place, but when the young trooper was led to one of the small, stunted trees and stripped to the waist, she started forward.

"What are you doing? What's happening?" she cried, although the preparations told her all too plainly what was about to take place.

"Field punishment," Sergeant Wright told her curtly. "Shall I send the prisoner to the rear?" he asked.

"No," replied Captain Ward, biting off the word savagely. "Being the cause of the trooper betraying his trust, it's only right that she should see the consequences – make sure she does."

Johnnie Gray's wrists were tried to a branch above his head, and stepping forward the sergant took off his own belt and twisted the buckle end about his hand before looking towards the officer.

"Eight strokes," said Captain Ward, his voice even.

Anstey closed her eyes, to open them again as a hand closed in her hair and her head was jerked by the soldier who held her. "*Watch*, the officer said," he told her, his voice rough, and against her will she did, as stroke after stroke of what looked like red paint appeared on the smooth white back.

At first Johnnie clenched his teeth and was silent, but at last his resolve gave way and he uttered a high-pitched whimper, reminding Anstey of a beaten dog. Wrenching herself free, she darted forward to seize the sergeant's upraised arm.

"No!" she cried. "No more – he's had enough."

Sergeant Wright seemed nonplussed, looking over her head to Captain Ward for guidance.

"His punishment isn't complete," he was told.

Anstey wrung her hands, almost crying in her distress. "It was my fault – I should be the one to be punished."

"Very well – then take his place."

Catching her breath, she stared up the officer, reading satisfaction in his expression at her startled reaction. She realized suddenly that it pained him to have his trooper beaten, whereas it would disturb him not at all to inflict the same punishment on her.

Slowly turning her head, she looked at the figure of the trooper hanging from the tree, silent now save for an occasional whimper like a tired child.

"Well, which is it be?" demanded the soldier harshly. "You or the boy?"

Taking a shaking breath, she lifted her chin and faced him defiantly. "Me," she said clearly.

There was a murmur among the ranks of the troopers, stirring them like a wind among trees.

"Remove your coat," ordered the officer and she turned a pleading face in his direction, thinking he meant to strip her like the trooper. "Only your coat," he said, almost gently. "We haven't time for a peepshow."

Sliding her arms out of the sleeves, Anstey shivered in the sudden chill as she dropped the jacket on the grass at her feet.

"Carry on, Sergeant," Captain Ward ordered. "Two strokes are wanting, I think."

A rough hand twisted in the hair at the nape of her neck and Anstey almost cried out with fright, her flesh cringing at the thought of what was to come. The first blow knocked her to her knees, and remembering the bloody weals on Johnnie Gray's back, she was thankful for the protection provided by her waistcoat and shirt. Almost at once another blow pitched her forward on to her outstretched hands, and she barely suppressed a cry of pain as the heavy leather belt snaked about her shoulders.

Afraid to move, Anstey lay still, her face buried in the short grass, while the trooper was released and helped away by his friends. Boots tramped around her and she knew that the soldiers were preparing to move out. She was ignored and for a few wild moments she hoped she had been forgotten, but eventually hands seized her and her arms were thrust into the sleeves of her coat.

"Come on, miss," urged the sergeant gruffly, "time to mount up."

She was pushed into her saddle and Sergeant Wright reached over from his own mount to take the reins out of her hands.

"I'm to have charge of you, miss – you'll not find me so easy to bamboozle as Johnnie Gray."

Anstey looked at him. "I'm sorry," she said. "I didn't think he'd be in trouble."

"Then you should have. What did you think he'd get for aiding a prisoner to escape – a reward? It's a good thing Captain Ward's got a heart."

"He's a brute!"

"Gray could have been hanged for what he did," the sergant told her sternly, "and as for you, my cully, you just be thankful you was allowed to keep your shirt. I've known officers what would have been glad for the excuse to strip you off and have a bit of sport."

Shuddering, Anstey looked away and despite its ending, wished the journey over. Feeling something akin to hate welling in her as she caught sight of the English officer's straight figure astride his horse, a little to one side, watching his men form into a double column.

Satisfied that all was as it should be and that the prisoner and Trooper Gray were placed in the middle of the line of men, he nodded to the sergeant, who gave the order and once more they rode forward.

They had lost time and Fort Augustus, their destination for that night, was still many miles distant. Anstey was used to spending hours on horseback, but not to riding all day with only short halts to rest the horses, and soon began to feel infinitely weary. She stretched aching muscles and winced a little as her bruised shoulders protested. Aware that the sergeant's shrewd eyes were upon her, she straightened her back and lifted her head with an attempt at pride, but soon found herself drooping with tiredness.

"You all right, miss?" asked Sergeant Wright.

"Yes," she answered shortly and hooked her fingers tightly over the rim of the saddle.

For a while they jogged on, the steady pace eating up the miles. Anstey was scarcely aware of her surroundings, her back aching intolerably and her fingers cramped and cold from retaining their grip on the saddle pommel. A great weariness seemed to overtake her, her eyes closing of their own accord as she slumped forward.

The watchful man beside her caught her arm and called to the officer ahead.

"Prisoner's swooning," he said, as Captain Ward wheeled his horse and joined him on the other side of the girl.

An impersonal gloved hand pushed up her chin, and Anstey opened her eyes to find herself staring into a coldly indifferent gaze.

"Well?" he demanded.

"Well – w-what?" she returned, puzzled, meaning to speak normally, but her voice no more than a tired whisper.

"Are you like to swoon, as the sergeant claims?"

"No," she answered proudly, but he had already seen her pallor and reaching into his pocket produced a flask.

"Not your heathen national drink," he said, removing the top, "but good brandy."

Heedless of her faint protest, he tipped a small quantity between her lips and watched dispassionately as she choked a little and a faint tinge of colour returned to her cheeks.

"Take the lead," he said to Sergeant Wright. "I'll take guard of the prisoner for a while."

The reins were passed across, and with a brief salute the sergant cantered ahead. As they rode along Anstey was aware of the officer's gaze on her, and turning her head to meet his eyes, lifted her eyebrows interrogatively.

"I was thinking that you'll not be so foolish as to attempt to escape again – even though I would be wiser than to accept your word of honour, which obviously is a thing of very little value."

Anstey flushed and felt her anger flare. "I would make a bid for freedom at the very gates of London itself," she told him fiercely, her voice harsh and strained. "Don't think you'll have an easy job conveying me to your masters, for I intend to make it as difficult as possible."

Captain Ward smiled and settled in his saddle as though satisfied. "I thought so," he said quietly, and Anstey stared at him, appalled by the ease with which she had fallen into the trap set for her. "From now on, Miss Frazer, you'll find your journey a great deal more uncomfortable. And don't think to gain my sympathy by acting a fainting fit, for I'll have no compunction in tying your ankles together under the belly of your mount and so prevent your falling off."

"I would not expect to gain your sympathy in any way," Anstey exclaimed, "for I know you have none . . . nor kindness or humanity, or any kind of gentlemanly feeling whatsoever. You are totally despicable and cruel and – and I hate you, for the harsh, unfeeling creature you are!"

He leaned closer. "Hate away, mistress," he told her, "for I care not for your opinion of me, only for getting you to London and there being rid of you."

Anstey grew cold at mention of London and all it implied, closing her eyes against a sudden picture of a jeering crowd and a waiting hangman. She swayed in the saddle and felt her arm taken in a hard grip as she was jerked upright.

"Dammit, woman, sit up, or I'll carry out my threat."

Straightening herself, she shook off his hand. "Your threats, Captain Ward, leave me quite unmoved," she told him defiantly, for all her voice was weary. "Best by far to have a care for your command, for I tell you freely that I intend to make your life miserable and your duty impossible."

As he met the challenge in her eyes his brows drew together, before he gave a snort of scornful laughter. "I should have thought you would have learned your lesson earlier and ridden south like a defeated lamb."

She shook her head. "The only lesson I learned was not to admit defeat – I'll fight with the last breath in my body – so be warned."

His expression was cruel. "Not a well-chosen phrase, Miss Frazer," he pointed out. "A little too apt to be comfortable, I would have thought."

Her fingers closed tightly upon the leather of the saddle and she turned quickly away so that he might not have the satisfaction of seeing the pain and terror he had raised.

"Have you a sister or wife, Captain Ward?" she asked, keeping her voice firm by an effort of will. "A loved one, perhaps, if you can find it in that cold heart of yours to feel affection for another? Then, Captain Ward, I hope that such a one never has such as you to taunt and injure her. I pray that she has a kinder fate than I."

"Pshaw, histrionics, Miss Frazer! If I am unkind then it's because of your murderous deed, and if fate is against you, then you have only yourself to blame. I have no wife, but my sister, thank God, is a civilised, gentle creature and could never find it in herself to hurt an insect, let alone a man."

Anstey turned her head and studied him quietly. "I think you might find her different if her country were invaded and her home and family threatened."

"Make me no excuses," she was told coldly. "There can be none for the killing of such as Leo Smythe. I knew him well and know beyond any doubt that he was not capable of attacking you as you suggest." He ran his eye over her, taking in her slim form and dark eyes. "I happen to know that he ever had a preference for blonde, Junoesque women. I cannot believe that his tastes would have changed so radically since his wife died that he would have taken a violent desire for a female of your colouring and size."

Flushing under his clearly disparaging gaze Anstey bit her lip and looked away, refusing to be drawn on the subject of the death of Captain Smythe. Instead she ignored the man beside her, withdrawing into her own thoughts, and so was surprised when she lifted her head some time later to find that they were descending from the mountains and approaching a long strip of water, which she recognised from her visits to the town at its head as Loch Ness.

Ahead of them lay the fort built to subdue the Highlands after the abortive Jacobite rising of 1715 – which General Wade had used as his quarters while building the roads which would make such a task easier. She had passed the little square of buildings many times before without a glance, but now her heart fell as she and her escort left the road, turning aside to enter the compound and the heavy wooden doors closed behind them.

CHAPTER
THREE

ANSTEY was lodged in the Governor's house and, for
the first time for many days, offered the luxury of a
bedroom and hot water for her toilet. Governor Martin's wife made no effort to hide her shocked disap-
proval of Anstey's attire and hastened to make her the
offer of the loan of one of her daughter's gowns,
insisting that she and her husband were not barbarians
and would expect the prisoner to dine with them that
night. Anstey could not resist stealing a glance at
Captain Ward to see how he was taking such a command, but found his face carefully blank.

"I fear that Captain Ward would not approve," she
demurred.

"I have very little feelings upon the matter," he
hastened to say, "save that with you under my eyes I
might feel a little easier in my mind." He turned to
Mrs. Martin and bowed. "Although she may look far
from it, the prisoner is dangerous, having already
killed one man, and has told me clearly that she has
every intention of attempting to escape – if you still
feel you wish for such as she at your table, I shall be
happy to guard both you," he turned and gave Anstey
a glance of chilly warning, "and her," he finished,
pointedly.

Mrs. Martin studied the girl, her face troubled, and

then her expression cleared. "Ah, well," she said, "I dare say that with two armed men in the room we shall be quite safe – besides, we so rarely see any visitors that I should be sorry to miss one."

Anstey smiled. "I assure you I shall be on my best behaviour and shall give you no cause for alarm," she said, and was escorted upstairs to her room by a trooper.

Opening the door a few minutes later, she found him standing a few yards away, obviously on guard, and realizing the position she gave him a pleasant smile before closing the door again. Knowing that there was no means of escape in that direction, she gave her attention to the window and finding it not only small but nailed firmly closed, gave up all thoughts of escape for the moment, instead concentrating upon enjoying the luxury of a lengthy wash and clean feminine clothes.

The dress put out for her was a pale pink silk with a modest hoop to hold out the full skirts and to her pleasure fitted her tolerably well. The elderly maid lent to her by Mrs. Martin coaxed her hair into curls with the aid of hot tongs, and when at last she entered the dining room Anstey felt a different woman from the bedraggled, grubby waif in male disguise who had entered the fort a few hours previously.

All eyes were turned upon her as she paused in the doorway and then the Governor came forward to lead her to the fire that burned brightly at one end of the room. Making her curtseys, Anstey looked fully at the Redcoat, pausing deliberately long enough for him to be forced to give her his hand to raise her. Releasing her as soon as he could, he pointedly turned his shoul-

der and spoke to his hostess, but Anstey had already
seen the surprise in his grey eyes and knew to her
satisfaction that her appearance had shaken him.

Lifting her chin, she engaged the Governor in conversation, setting out to make herself vivacious and
attractive, using every wile she possessed to please
him. Once or twice she was aware that James Ward
was watching her and knew that her behaviour was
making him uneasy, knowing too that she was rapidly
losing Mrs. Martin as an ally.

Exhilarated by wine and food and comfort, Anstey
wished the evening could go on for ever, but almost
before she was aware of the passing hours, the candles
were guttering and Captain Ward was excusing himself and his prisoner on the grounds of the long journey before them.

"I'll ring for an escort for Miss Frazer," offered
Governor Martin.

"No need at the moment," returned the officer,
"but I'd be grateful for a guard to be placed outside
her room all night."

Making graceful thanks Anstey took her leave and
was a little disconcerted to find that the Englishman
intended to escort her upstairs.

"I can hardly make an escape from so closely
guarded an establishment as this," she pointed out
reasonably. "Besides, I am much too tired to attempt
anything so energetic."

"Then let us hope that Governor Martin ignores the
invitation you so clearly gave him and does not disturb
you tonight," the soldier said evenly, making her gasp
with outrage.

"You are insulting, sir!" she cried, pausing on the

staircase to glare at him, to her chagrin well aware that she had behaved badly that evening, and only dimly aware that she had been prompted by a wish to prove herself still attractive after the rigours and unconcealed dislike that had accompanied the journey from Cushlan Keep.

"Then don't behave like a jade if you don't wish to be treated like one," he told her giving her an impatient little push in the direction of her chamber.

His action was too much for Anstey's over-strained nerves; rounding on him with her fingers crooked, she scored her nails down his cheek.

"Explain that away, Sassenach," she said, viewing the three red scratches with satisfaction.

" I shall tell any who ask that I was attacked by a wild cat." The Englishman took out a handkerchief and dabbed his bleeding cheek with composure, only the roughness with which he took her shoulder and turned her towards her room betraying his anger.

Feeling her flinch under his grasp, his eyes narrowed and a thin smile curved his mouth as his hand slid across her shoulders in a gesture that was almost a caress.

"Next time I'll punish you myself," he warned softly, "and you'll not find my touch so light as the sergeant's."

Twitching herself away from him, Anstey almost ran to her room, hearing his soft chuckle float along the dark corridor behind her. Closing the door, she leaned against it for one minute, her heart hammering against her tight bodice, and more afraid of the Redcoat than she cared to admit. The thought of the long journey ahead filled her with disquiet and apprehension, knowing that by her own nature, which had never been docile, she must antagonise the soldier even while she dreaded the outcome of such a clash. Comforting herself with the thought of the little knife which Catlin had slipped into her boot at the croft, she climbed into bed and spent a restless, wakeful night, only falling heavily asleep as dawn began to light her room.

After the voluminous skirts and petticoats of the night before, to return to male attire seemed more embarrassing than ever, and deeply conscious of her legs in their revealing green breeches, Anstey stepped out on to the parade ground the next morning, feeling that all eyes were upon her, leering and ogling.

However, no one took the slightest notice of her, all appearing busy about their own affairs, strapping equipment on to the pack horses or burnishing accoutrements in a last-minute effort before inspection. To Anstey their red coats and powdered hair seemed strangely unreal, and she had to remind herself that under the stiff uniforms were men, much like any other save that they were English and invaders of her country.

"This way, miss," said her escort, and led her towards a wooden shack open to the air on three sides in one corner of the compound.

Captain Ward and the Sergeant turned at her approach, something in their expressions making the pit of her stomach contract with anticipation.

"Come in, Miss Frazer," said the Captain as she hesitated, "we're ready for you."

Warily Anstey searched his face, but reading only blandness there turned her attention on the Sergeant who tipped his hat and nodded. At last she looked at the third man, who by his dress and huge stature could only be a smith, and seeing that which he held in his gnarled hands, she turned cold with horror and started back.

"No!" she cried, sending a look of entreaty towards the impassive officer.

"Yes," he returned and she bit her lip on further appeals, knowing their futility. "Pray present your wrists," he went on, "and be warned that if you move while the smith is bending the irons to fit, he may well break your arm with his hammer."

"Come on, miss," said Sergeant Wright with rough kindliness. "Kneel down and it'll soon be over."

Leaning over her, he held her arms on the anvil as the smith slipped the open iron rings over her hands and closed them with a few smart blows. A chain was passed between them and padlocked in place.

"There, it didn't take long," observed Captain Ward levelly as he pocketed the key, his voice sounding to Anstey like one who had ordered a chain for a dog.

Scrambling to her feet, she faced him proudly, heedless of the single tear of shame that trickled down her cheek. "I h-hate you," she said, her voice shaking. "One day you'll pay for this —"

"Miss Frazer, I grow weary of your threats," he said, taking a pinch of snuff with a studiedly elegant air. "Truth to tell, they leave me quite indifferent — as do you."

So saying he strolled away, leaving Anstey to stare after his tall back, black hate overcoming any fear she had felt previously.

"Oh, if only I were a man –" she raged uselessly, stamping a foot and quivering with temper.

"Well, you're not – and be thankful you aren't," said the Sergeant's voice from behind her. "For if you was, you'd have a sore back by now."

Anstey shot him an eloquent glance.

"Lor' love you – that wasn't no more than a tickle you had yesterday." He sobered suddenly and moved closer to lower his voice and say confidingly, "If you'd take my advice, miss, you'd stop this tantalising and teasing of Captain Ward. He's been very patient so far, but his temper when aroused isn't pleasant – not nice to see, if you take my meaning, and even worse to be on the receiving end of it."

Anstey lifted her chin, and suddenly aware of the drying tear raised her hand to brush it impatiently away, making her chain rattle as she did so. Catching her breath, she glanced down at her steel bracelets before meeting the Sergeant's eyes boldly.

"I am not afraid of Captain Ward," she told him, her voice high and carrying. "Indeed I regard him as a brute and a bully, nothing more."

"Then you are more foolish than I thought you," said Sergeant Wright stolidly, and taking her arm led her to her horse.

Only her spur of resentment and her refusal to lower her pride allowed Anstey to endure the interminable journey of that day, as they rode past Cluny Castle and on towards the Pass of Killiecrankie. With each hour new aches seemed to attack her tired body and with each jog of her mount the handcuffs on her wrists rubbed and chafed until her skin was red and sore. That night they sheltered in a rude croft, crowded together in its smoky confines. Anstey's bed was a pile of heather in one corner, but so tired was she that her head was nodding even as she attempted to eat the rough stew the soldiers had cooked, and somewhat to her surprise she did not wake until morning.

Johnnie Gray was kept well away from her, but Anstey was relieved to see that he seemed none the worse for his ordeal and appeared to bear her no ill will, for he smiled surreptitiously in her direction when she caught his eye.

The weather until then had been good, but as though to make up for its previous clemency they set off into a grey morning with the nearby valleys and mountains shrouded in thick mist that hid the sun and struck chill to man and horse.

As the day wore on, contrary to their expectations, the weather grew worse, the mist imperceptibly creeping lower until the path they were following vanished into a blank whiteness a few yards ahead. During their journey the track had gradually risen, winding its way up the mountainside, and now as they rode in single file, stones dislodged by their passing rolled down the steep slope that edged the path, falling into the hidden valley below with a dull finality that made Anstey watch the narrow road uneasily.

They had just passed a widening in the road, a semi-circular hollow in the rock that rose above them, when disaster happened. Captain Ward had taken the opportunity of relieving the Sergeant of the task of guarding Anstey and had ridden on in the rain, leading her behind him, when the treacherous path began to crumble beneath their horses feet. With a shout he urged the animals to effort and speed and reached safety as the track behind them broke away from the mountainside and plunged down the precipice to crash into the valley.

For a moment Anstey could do nothing more than slide from her mount's back and stare down into the enveloping mist at her feet, picturing what her fate would have been but for the quick action of the Redcoat.

The figures of the other soldiers could be dimly made out on the far side of the gap, peering anxiously across.

"You all right, sir?" came the Sergeant's strident tones.

"Yes, we're both safe." Dismounting, James Ward walked to the edge of the torn pathway and took stock of the situation. "We can't get back until this mist lifts," he said.

"We can make camp in the opening back a bit – but what about you? All the food and equipment is this side."

"We'll find shelter for the night and meet up again in the morning. I give the troop into your command, Sergeant."

For a while they could hear muffled sounds of the soldiers' departure, but these were quickly lost in the heavy mist which seemed to blanket off noise, wrapping them individually in silence and damp.

Captain Ward turned to Anstey. "Well, Miss Frazer," he said, looming over her, a black figure wrapped in his thick cloak beaded with drops of moisture, "we'd best set about finding some means of shelter. Stay here while I go on a little."

Anstey watched him disappear into the mist and feeling more alone than she had ever done, fell to petting the horses for company. The Captain returned sooner than she expected, his boots crunching on the gravel path.

"There's a cave not far on," he announced. "We'll take the horses to provide us with warmth."

Taking the reins he led the animals away, apparently assuming that Anstey would follow, and after hesitating for a second, she stumbled after him. The path widened shortly and soon they came to the cave which was little more than a fissure in the rock, being fairly narrow and extremely high, its sides stretching away into the mist overhead. The Captain tied the horses near the entrance and peremptorily ordered Anstey to search for wood while he attempted to kindle a fire.

Soon acrid smoke began to drift around the cave, held low by the heavy air. The damp wood refused to do more than smoulder despite the Englishman's best efforts, and provided little warmth.

Anstey remained near the entrance, huddled on a boulder, hugging her cloak about her and staring out into the enveloping mist.

"Come to the fire – such as it is," said a quiet voice behind her as a deep shudder of cold shook her.

"I prefer it here," she answered, not turning her head.

"Afraid, Miss Frazer?" James Ward enquired, softly. "Are you nervous that I might take advantage of your late offer?"

Anstey looked at him coldly. "If I had offered you what you suppose, I would hardly be nervous of your accepting it," she pointed out and to show how little she feared him, moved nearer the smouldering wood and held her hands to the dim red glow. As she did so, her shackles rattled dismally and she hurriedly dropped her arms and hid them among the folds of her cloak.

"I have some biscuit in my saddlebag," observed the soldier. "With that and my brandy flask we shall manage."

"I'm not hungry," Anstey told him as he rummaged in the leather bag and set out hard biscuit upon his handkerchief.

"It's better than it looks – try it."

"I don't want any."

"Do as you're told, Miss Frazer," he said lazily, munching his own portion. "I've no wish for you to fall ill in this God-forsaken country."

"And I've no wish to leave it," she cried, glaring at him. "I would sooner by far fall ill and die here, than be taken to London to entertain the crowds upon Tower Hill!"

"I dare say – but to London you'll go, whether you wish or not – even if I have to drag you there."

For a moment they glowered at each other, the red scratches on the soldier's cheek very plain as he leaned forward to push a biscuit in Anstey's direction.

"Eat it," he commanded.

Anstey lifted her chin. "You can't make me," she said.

He eyed her coldly, "I remember my nurse holding my nose until I'd swallowed," he began, but suddenly struck by the ludicrous situation abruptly abandoned it. "Very well," he conceded. "Starve if you like, but expect no consideration from me when you feel faint."

Anstey could have remarked that she had received very little consideration from any of her escort, but instead maintained a lofty silence as she hunched a shoulder and tried to find a comfortable spot upon the hard, pebble-strewn floor.

A heavy silence fell, broken only by the occasional sound from the horses as they chewed their bits and shifted position. Anstey was uncomfortably aware that the soldier was watching her, and after a while he spoke.

"What is your story of Leo Smythe's death?" he asked unexpectedly.

Anstey stiffened. "I have none," she said shortly.

"Tell me what happened."

"If you are curious you have only to read the official report, which no doubt you carry among your despatches."

"I'd like to hear your version."

"I don't wish to talk about it."

"Squeamish, Miss Frazer?"

She looked at him then. "It's not every day I kill a man," she told him, stung.

"You surprise me – from your manner, I would have supposed it quite a usual occurrence. Tell me what happened."

"No!"

"You were in your house and the soldiers rode up. Were you alone?"

"No – *yes*."

He raised his eyebrows. "Don't you know?"

"Of course I do. I meant I was alone except for the servants who were in a different part of the house."

"Very concise, Miss Frazer, so clear that one would almost suppose it rehearsed, in fact!" James Ward watched her hands slowly clench upon themselves before he went on. "And your brother, and this beautiful sister of yours, where were they?"

"Out."

"Where?" he asked inexorably.

"M-my brother was hunting – and my sister was visiting an old servant. I was alone. I shot your friend, Captain Ward, with a pistol of my father's." She took a shuddering breath and choked back a sound which might have been a sob. "I – will not talk about it any more," she said wearily, and rested her head upon her hands.

The Englishman watched her thoughtfully, a frown between his brows. "Is it a custom to keep a loaded pistol in the drawing-room?" he wondered.

"Only when there is the possibility of a visit from an enemy army," she answered bitterly, after a perceptible pause which the Englishman was quick to notice.

"And your brother and sister – where are they now?"

Anstey lifted her head from her hands to send him a swift glance. "You heard me tell Sir Robert; they are safe, Jamie is in France by now and Isobel is with our old nurse."

"Jamie, now – how old is he?"

Rising abruptly, she crossed to the entrance and leaning against one rocky wall, looked out into the damp, shrouded world beyond the cave. "I won't talk about it," she said, "I told you—"

"I was under the impression that your brother was the subject of our conversation, which is quite different . . . is it not?"

Anstey was forced to nod reluctant agreement and her companion went on evenly.

"Then come back to the fire and tell me about him."

"Why?" she asked, turning.

Captain Ward shrugged. "Why not? – Politics are a banned subject, my army exploits would not interest you and I have no idea of your interests."

Seating herself once more on the hard floor, Anstey cupped her chin in her hands and resting her elbows on her knees, gazed into the weak flames that licked the damp wood.

"How old is he?" persisted the Redcoat and she answered almost automatically, her mind elsewhere.

"Fourteen."

"Almost an adult."

Straightening quickly, she flung him a startled glance. "Not at all! Jamie is a boy – he's young for his age. A mere child."

The Captain's eyes were shrewd and alert and seeing his interest in her over-reaction to his words, Anstey, casting about for some means of distracting him, did the only thing that occurred to her and leaping to her feet, kicked the fire in his direction and plunged desperately towards the cave entrance.

The horses tossed and jostled, losing her precious seconds, and before she could slip past them, her shoulder was seized and she was thrust roughly backwards to lose her footing and fall headlong. Squirming away from the hands that reached for her, Anstey remembered the *sgian dubh* in her boot and snatched the deadly little knife out of hiding, as she scrambled to her feet.

Captain Ward's eyes narrowed at sight of her weapon, and after an imperceptible pause, he approached her cautiously.

"What do you hope to achieve with that?" he asked scornfully. "It's no better use than a penknife."

"Our little knives have accounted for many an English soldier," she reminded him, facing him warily, her arms outstretched and ready to strike.

Even as her words echoed about the cave, he was upon her, bearing her backwards with his weight and pinning her to the ground while he held her manacled hands that grasped the *sgian dubh* above her head.

"Drop it, Miss Frazer," he commanded coolly, "or I'll hurt you."

For answer Anstey struggled wildly, twisting her body and hitting and scratching with her free hand. His fingers tightened about her wrist as he stared down into her face.

"Drop it," he repeated, ignoring her efforts for freedom.

For answer Anstey clawed at his face. Jerking his head back, he smiled into her eyes and slowly exerted his strength until she thought her wrist would snap. Biting her lip against the pain, she turned her head away and heard the knife fall from her numbed fingers.

Catching up the chain between her handcuffs the soldier dragged her to her feet, sending the *sgian dubh* out of the cave with a well-aimed kick.

"Enough!" he said roughly, flinging her down

beside the remains of the fire. "One move out of you and I'll truss you like a chicken ready for the spit. Be warned, wench, my patience is at an end – and I'm hard put to keep my hands off you."

He stood over her and stared wrathfully down. "Are there any more weapons about you?"

Hugging her wrist, Anstey gave a small shake of her head.

"I know that your word is not worth the breath used to give it – shall I search you?"

Anstey turned a white face up to him. "Truly I have nothing," she said breathlessly, and showed her hands palms outwards in an unconsciously appealing gesture.

Taking in her pallor and barely-controlled trembling, the Captain gave a slight nod. "Try no tricks," he advised, "for I intend to sleep with your chain in my hand . . . and I am not in the mood for gentleness."

Looking at his tight mouth and grim expression Anstey could believe him, and made herself small while he banked up the fire and settled himself beside her for the night. True to his word, he reached out for her chain, taking it in one strong brown hand, before he closed his eyes and appeared to fall quickly asleep.

Anstey rubbed her wrist and allowed herself the luxury of weeping silently. Although weary beyond measure she was unable to relax, and stared at the fire until it burned low, her mind filled with thoughts and fears. At last her eyes closed and she fell asleep to awake in the early light of dawn. One quick glance told her that the cave was empty save for the horses, and kicking aside the cloak which covered her she leaped to her feet just as the Redcoat appeared in the entrance.

"There's a little stream below the road," he told her, by his expression well aware of her thoughts. "I'll give you ten minutes for your toilet."

Wondering at his apparent lack of interest in her movements, Anstey climbed down to the running water and looking about her, realized why; for a good distance in either direction the view was clear and uninterrupted. It would take anyone far more than ten minutes to find shelter in that empty landscape.

Her toilet complete, she was climbing back to the cave when the clatter of hooves made her look at the road above to see a trooper riding up.

"We found another track over the mountain, sir," he said, "and the troop is waiting up ahead."

"Well done. Ride back and tell Sergeant Wright that we are on our way." Captain Ward glanced down at Anstey. "Come along, Miss Frazer, time to resume our journey," he said.

Obediently Anstey mounted her horse, keeping her head bent with an air of submission she was far from feeling; by a coincidence, when the Redcoat had kicked her knife out of the cave it had fallen into the shallow stream below where she had just found it, and now it was nestling snugly in her boot again.

CHAPTER
FOUR

THAT morning they dropped down into the Pass of Killiecrankie where the battle between the English soldiers and Highlanders had taken place over fifty years before, and so wild and threatening a spot was it, with high towering cliffs, their steep sides split by narrow fissures, that Anstey could well believe all the ghastly tales she had heard about its ghostly inhabitants. The troopers who rode with her were not impervious to its lowering atmosphere, and loosening their weapons they rode warily, alert for trouble.

They reached the cathedral city of Dunkeld that evening and set off towards Perth the next morning, with Anstey so bone-weary and aching from the long ride that she felt scarcely rested after the night's halt. Even though so tired that she hunched in her saddle taking little notice of her surroundings, yet the countryside was so different to her familiar north-west Highlands, that she raised her head and glanced about, surprised by the thickly wooded slopes and astonished to note the size and luxuriant foliage after the few bent and stunted trees to which she was accustomed.

Although they were so much further south the road was empty of travellers other than themselves, and save for a few tiny crofts there was little sign of habitation on these hospitable mountainsides.

The soldiers, feeling that they had left the dangerous part of the journey behind and that they were nearing civilization and home, relaxed their watch and rode more easily, chatting quietly among themselves, so that when the attack came the surprise was complete and set them milling in confusion, until the officer's carrying tones ordered them to scatter and seek shelter.

Anstey, who was as surprised as any, felt her bridle seized as her horse was urged at a gallop off the exposed road and into the shelter of the trees that bounded it.

"Get down out of sight," commanded Captain Ward, pushing her out of the saddle as he dismounted himself and looked round to see how his men fared.

Hiding herself behind a tree-trunk, Anstey watched as he dashed from man to man at a crouching run, stopping only to make certain they were unhurt and setting about the lengthy business of priming their pistols before dashing on to the next man in his journey to find a vantage point and discover the whereabouts of their assailants.

"They're over among the trees yonder," said a voice beside Anstey, and she turned her head to find the Sergeant sharing her tree. "Your countrymen of course, and after our weapons, I'll be bound."

A volley of shots whistled over their heads, making them duck as the balls spent themselves against the tree-trunks or were lost among the leaves and branches.

"I'll look to the men – but don't think you can slip

away, for I'll give them the word to keep their eyes on you."

Sergeant Wright touched her warningly on the shoulder, before he moved away with a quick litheness that surprised her. Peering out from behind her shelter, she saw a splash of red a few yards from the road lying on the space where the encroaching trees had been cleared. By stretching her neck, she could make out that it was one of the soldiers and even as she stared at him, he moved his head feebly and she recognized the boyish features of Johnnie Gray. He appeared to be holding his thigh with both hands, where a bright red blotch stained his white breeches. As she watched his head fell back and he lay still, his hands spread at his sides.

Looking about, Anstey realized that there was no one nearby to help; each soldier was intent upon his orders and too far away to aid her. From gossip and talk she knew that such hurts could be extremely dangerous and that a man could bleed to death from a wound in the thigh unless it was attended to quickly. Anstey waited no longer, but jumping to her feet ran out of the surrounding trees and headed for the fallen soldier.

She thought she heard shouts from behind, but taking no notice she sped over the grass tufts and fallen branches until she reached the trooper, and could fling herself down beside him. One look at his white face, with the sheen of sweat upon it, told her that she was not a moment too soon, and for want of a bandage she tore her cravat from her neck, cut it raggedly in half with the aid of her *sgian dubh*, and managed to tie it above the welling blood, despite the handcuffs which restricted her movements. The little knife served also to thrust into the makeshift bandage and turn until the bright arterial blood ceased pumping. From her old nurse's teaching she knew that the tourniquet must not be applied too long for fear of cutting off the supply to the rest of the limb and causing gangrene, so after a few minutes she cautiously eased the binding and, relieved to see that the red stream had slowed to a trickle, used the other half of her cravat to cover the gaping bullet wound in Johnnie Gray's leg.

Suddenly becoming aware of shouts and the clash of steel which had been going on for some minutes in the forest on the far side of the road, she looked up in time to see the soldiers from behind her charge across the intervening ground and run into the trees opposite. Blood-chilling shouts and yells filled her with apprehension and she watched anxiously to see who would emerged the victor.

Slowly, red-coated figures began to appear in a desultory fashion, and she knew with a fall of her heart that her fellow-countrymen had been defeated. Sheathing their swords the soldiers crossed the road and gathered round her to stare down at the supine form of their comrade. With presence of mind Anstey had quickly replaced her knife in her boot at their approach, and was almost certain that none of them had seen her action.

"Make way, lads," commanded the Sergeant, pushing his way through and quickly summing up the situation. "There's nothing to be done here – off you go and find the horses."

The men obeyed him, and as he dropped on one

knee beside the fallen trooper, Captain Ward joined them and watched as the other man examined Anstey's rough bandage.

"I see you know something of doctoring," he said.

"Only what my nurse taught me. I know that a man can bleed to death from a wound in the thigh."

"He's you to thank for his life, miss," the Sergeant said soberly, his hands busy at the knots she had tied.

"Construct a litter, Sergeant," said the officer, and slipping a hand under Anstey's arm, lifted her to her feet and led her aside. "I'll take the knife, Miss Frazer, if you please," he said, pleasantly, holding out a hand.

"What knife?" demanded Anstey, her eyes wide and innocent.

James Ward sighed. "The one you used to cut your cravat," he told her, his gaze impervious.

Anstey eyed him reflectively but, reading the growing signs of impatience in his grey eyes, gave in abruptly and reaching down to her boot, put the *sgian dubh* in its neat leather sheath into his hand.

"Are you learning sense at last?" he wondered aloud, pocketing the tiny knife.

"More like I have learned that you are no gentleman," Anstey retorted, turning away as the men returned with the horses and were immediately put to the task of cutting branches to make a litter that could be slung between two animals and so carry the injured man to Perth.

The excitement of the short-lived fight and her efforts to save Johnnie Gray had buoyed her up, but once back in the saddle and jogging along the road again, all Anstey's crushing weariness returned and the handcuffs chafed her wrists until their painful irritation could no longer be ignored. By the time they stopped for their mid-day meal, she viewed the bread and cheese offered her with tired indifference, the iron bracelets she wore making every movement an ordeal.

"Best eat your food, miss," said Sergeant Wright. "We've still a way to go."

"I don't want it," Anstey told him, pushing the meal away. The lace ruffles on her shirtcuffs fell back as she did so, revealing her sore and swollen wrists to the soldiers' interested gaze.

Surprisingly gentle fingers took her hands and the Sergeant turned them about to examine her wrists. Pursing his lips he said nothing, but a short while after he left, Captain Ward confronted her.

"The Sergeant tells me your handcuffs are giving you trouble," he said.

Anstey nodded. "Take them off," she half whispered, adding so quietly that the soldier was not sure he heard, "*Please.*"

Without a word the Captain possessed himself of her wrists and examined them as the other man had done. Feeling her flinch under his touch, he looked up briefly before releasing her hands.

"Please," she said again, very conscious that it was the first time she had asked the Englishman for anything and looking up, allowed her eyes to plead for her.

"With your countrymen so obviously spoiling for a fight, I want no possibility of your escape. You have yourself to blame if I cannot accept your word. I am afraid you'll have to bear your discomfort a while longer, Miss Frazer."

He spoke curtly and left her abruptly to confer with the Sergeant before ordering his men to finish their hurried meal and mount up in order to get their wounded comrade to a doctor in Perth with all speed possible.

A trooper was sent ahead to rouse the doctor and have a bed made ready in an inn, while the main column hurried as best they could for fear of starting the bleeding afresh. Anstey rode slumped in the saddle, too tired to lift her head, and the sore throat which had been threatening for several days grew worse with each mile, until it took all her concentration to remain on her mount. She was aware that the Sergeant rode watchfully near and was vaguely grateful for his presence, but by the time they neared the ancient capital and the broad expanse of the Tay, her world had shrunk until it only contained her weary body and the need to exert the last of her strength in an effort to stay in the saddle.

The ferry crossing was made and then she was dimly aware that they had halted and that Johnnie Gray was being taken into a hostelry, and then that someone had taken her bridle and that she alone was being led on across the road.

"Dismount, if you please, Miss Frazer."

Anstey made a move to comply, but her weary limbs refused to obey her, and after a moment hands reached up and pulled her from the saddle to stand her on her stiff legs. Swaying with exhaustion, she reached up and took hold of the white sword-belt that crossed the red coat in front of her and, giving a weary sigh, let her head droop slowly until her forehead nestled against Captain Ward's chest.

For a moment he looked down with a curious expression at the brown head resting against him, and for a pause in time he was oddly still before his hands closed slowly upon her shoulders, his grip firm and comforting.

A welcome feeling of security washed through Anstey and she allowed herself to lean upon his strength until she abruptly recalled whose chest it was she rested against and whose arms held her so pleasantly. Flinging back her head, she stared up into the Englishman's face, her own eyes wide and startled, before she pushed him away from her, and took a hasty step back.

She was free almost at her first movement. Captain Ward's expression was enigmatic as his hands fell to his sides. Behind him a fire roared and flared, the red light gleaming on a half-naked man, who worked a pair of bellows with immense concentration.

"W-where are we?"

He was quick to note the nervous query in her voice. "Not the devil's workshop, as you might suppose," he answered reassuringly. "It's a forge, and the smith here will strike off your irons."

Anstey looked at him quickly.

"I have reconsidered my refusal to release you this morning – and think perhaps my decision was a little harsh," he went on, leading her forward. "We are well out of your Highlands now, and besides—" he ran a practical eye over her drooping figure, "I think you have not the urge or will to attempt to escape at the moment."

Once freed from her fetters, she and James Ward walked back to the inn, where Anstey was handed into the care of a trooper and locked into a bedchamber, especially selected by the astute Sergeant for its impregnability. For once not interested in the possibility of escape, Anstey dropped on to the narrow bed and was asleep almost at once.

She was awoken by a loud knocking at the door and opened her eyes reluctantly, struggling through layers of sleep to consciousness.

"The Captain's compliments, miss, and I was to ask you to dinner," said the young Redcoat in the doorway.

Anstey blinked and rubbed her eyes, wishing nothing so much as to fall asleep again. "My thanks," she returned, "but I want nothing."

"Begging your pardon, miss, but it wasn't a request – more like an order, if you see what I mean."

"I do, trooper, I do indeed." Wearily she pushed herself to her feet and smoothed her hair in front of the pitted looking-glass on the wall. "Doubtless if I refuse you will carry me by force to the Captain's dining-table."

The soldier looked embarrassed. "I wasn't to take 'no' for an answer, the Captain said," he agreed, and went on a little hesitantly as they left the room and descended the steep stairs, "The lads, miss, wanted me to say we was grateful-like, for what you did for Johnnie Gray. He'd have died, else."

Anstey looked at him, her eyes dark pools of shadow. "I'm glad I could help him," she told him soberly. "I've owed him something for the beating he took for me."

"Well, he's young and no doubt has an eye for a pretty face," the soldier told her, tapping at a door before opening it for her.

Captain Ward turned from his contemplation of the fire that burned brightly in the hearth with deference to the Scottish weather rather than the time of year and coming forward, proffered his arm.

Setting her fingers lightly on his sleeve, Anstey allowed him to lead her to the table and hold the chair for her while she seated herself, wondering somewhat at his formal manners.

"I noticed that you ate nothing today," he said, reading her thoughts, "and thought to make sure you take a good meal tonight. We still have a long way to our destination, and I would deliver you strong and well."

"How unfortunate if I should die upon the way," Anstey agreed drily, her voice a little hoarse from her sore throat.

"Take heart, Miss Frazer," said the Redcoat bracingly, "I've not lost a prisoner yet." He lifted the lids on the dishes and began serving the food.

Anstey had little appetite and watched the meat and vegetables mounting on her plate with some dismay. However, the wine soothed her inflamed throat and she drank eagerly while toying with her food.

"We should be in Stirling tomorrow," the Captain went on conversationally, "having passed through Glen Eagles on our way." He looked up suddenly and gave one of his rare smiles. "You Scots seem to have a propensity to romantic names."

"It comes from the Gaelic and means church – nothing to do with eagles, I'm afraid."

"Perhaps so – but you must admit that your names have an air about them. Applecross, for instance. Loch Maree and Liathach mountain."

"I'm glad you like some things belonging to my country."

"I like a great many things native to Scotland, Miss Frazer."

His voice and expression were sober and after a moment Anstey dropped her own eyes, inexplicably reminded of the instance earlier that day when she had lowered her defences and forgotten that the Englishman was an implacable enemy. A flush not totally due to the wine she had drunk warmed her cheeks, and she hurriedly made a display of attacking her meal.

Captain Ward watched her silently, well aware of the cause of her discomposure. "Eat your dinner," he said easily, as she showed signs of setting down her cutlery with most of the food still on her plate, "and I'll let you off the landlady's formidable Cloutie Pudden, which upon investigation seems to be first cousin to our Christmas pudding."

Anstey forced down a few more mouthfuls before resolutely putting down her knife and fork and watching while her companion demolished a good portion of the steaming pudding put before him.

"And now, Miss Frazer," he said as the table was cleared, "pray present to me your wrists."

Immediately Anstey defensively hid her hands in her lap, eyeing him apprehensively across the table.

"I wish to make sure – I have seen blood-poisoning result from even a small wound—"

"And you want me to reach London in good health – I know," she finished for him and wearily proffered her hands.

She shivered at his touch as he pushed back the lace cuffs of her shirt to reveal her raw wrists, the purple marks of his previous grip showing clearly. His eyes flickered at the sight of her bruises, but he said nothing, only sending for water and salves.

Quickly and efficiently he washed and bandaged her wrists, while Anstey surreptitiously watched his face as he went about his task. His powdered hair contrasted strangely with his tanned skin, his black eyebrows and lashes making his grey eyes seem pale by comparison. The shadows cast by the candles highlighted his thin nose and the long planes of his cheeks.

Looking up suddenly, he caught her examining gaze upon him and for a moment their eyes joined and held, before Anstey hastily looked away and he returned to his task.

That night Anstey lay upon her hard, narrow bed wishing for the sleep that eluded her and found herself wondering upon the colour of the Englishman's hair; black, she supposed if one was to judge by his eyebrows . . . or dark brown.

They left Perth in a downpour, taking the road through Glen Eagles in rain so heavy that the short, steep glen was almost obscured and they all sank into their thick frieze cloaks and rode in acute discomfort and misery. Riding without a break, they arrived at Stirling Castle wet and dispirited. Immediately Captain Ward was hurried away to make his report to the commander of the garrison, and Anstey locked in a cell.

With cold rivulets of water trickling down her back, she dropped her soaking cloak at her feet and took in her surroundings. The tiny slit that served to let in air and some light was set high in the wall, while a mean straw palliasse on a wooden frame was the only furniture.

The soldier who brought her a bowl of stew demanded her cloak, explaining that Captain Ward wanted it dried, but apart from that she saw no one until morning, when the same trooper brought breakfast of bread and ale. Her clothes had dried upon her and she awoke stiff and cold with the beginnings of a headache, and found herself inordinately glad to leave the inhospitable fortress behind. Glancing up at the huge, impregnable rock as they left the town behind, Anstey could admire its position and strength, recalling that Jacobites had besieged the fortress earlier, but could find no sorrow in her heart to be leaving.

The rain of the day before had left the road a surface of mud, in some places the track was washed away and they had to dismount and lead their horses. By the time they halted for the midday meal, a faint, watery sun had broken through the clouds and Anstey was grateful for the slight warmth as she sat on a boulder to eat the inevitable bread and cheese.

Captain Ward had seated himself nearby and she was intrigued to see him take a small package out of his pocket, break the seal and examine the contents, which appeared to be a locket of some kind before, holding it in his hand, he began to read the writing on the paper which had enclosed it. His reading appeared to afford him little pleasure, for his black brows drew together in a frown and his eyes having travelled to the bottom of the page, returned quickly to the top again as he began to read it anew.

Much interested, Anstey watched him surreptitiously, and when he dropped the locket as he rewrapped it in the paper, sprang to her feet before he could retrieve it and seized the little gold case. It had sprung open in its fall and she found herself staring at a beautiful face surrounded by fair hair. Delicate brows above vivid blue eyes and a red, curved mouth completed the picture.

"Isabel!" she gasped, raising a bewildered face to the Englishman. "What are you doing with a portrait of my sister?"

"Who do you say it is?" he asked slowly.

Anstey looked from him to the painted face in her hand, her brain working speedily. Now that she looked more closely, she could see small differences that made the likeness less, but at first glance it could have been her sister's face lying in her palm.

"Who is it?" she asked.

"Leo Smythe's wife."

With an audible gasp Anstey looked up quickly. "So *that's* why he—" she began, breaking off as she realized the inadvisability of her words.

"Why what, Miss Frazer?"

"Why – he said there was a likeness between his wife and my sister."

"I thought you said your sister was out when he came to your house."

"So she was," agreed Anstey hastily, realizing her mistake. "I meant a likeness to Isabel's portrait."

Grey eyes looked steadily down at her. "There seem to be enough paintings around to please any impecunious artist," he remarked drily, opening the locket as it was returned to him and studying the painted face with interest. "Strange that two women so far apart should be so alike," he mused.

"I daresay it's quite superficial, and if they were to be put side by side, one would see nothing out of the ordinary."

"Unfortunately we cannot put it to the test – Mrs. Smythe is dead, have you forgot?"

Anstey looked down at her muddy boots. "For the moment," she acknowledged.

"Why do you have the locket?" she asked, as they mounted and formed a double file.

"Leo had asked me previously to return it to his family if anything happened to him."

"And the babe – did it live?"

"Yes," he answered shortly and gave the order to move off.

"Where is it?"

The glance he shot her was a little intimidating. "Let me tell you, Miss Frazer, that I find your interest in the child of the man done to death at your hands, somewhat distasteful," he told her bluntly.

Flushing and biting her lip, Anstey tightened her hold on the reins and stared down at her hands. "I – only wondered if it was being cared for – loved," she said in a choked voice.

"As far as I know she is still in the house of her maternal grandmother," he said shortly, after a pause and urging his horse into a trot, left her and rode to the head of the column.

As though by mutual consent Anstey and James Ward avoided each other as much as possible for the rest of that day, but she was aware that his eyes often rested upon her with speculation in his grey gaze when he thought himself unobserved.

Late that afternoon they came upon a place where a

spring rushing out of the hillside above the road had washed the track away, leaving a slide of mud and shingle, covered by a few inches of flowing water.

"Dismount," ordered the Captain, "we'll have to lead the horses."

With the reins in her hand and the warmth of her horse at her shoulder, Anstey waited her turn, watching as the soldiers and animals splashed to where Captain Ward supervised the operation from the other side of the water.

"You next, miss," said Sergeant Wright. "Let your horse find his own way and look out for yourself."

Obediently she moved forward, holding the reins lightly and picking her way from boulder to boulder that showed above the muddy water. She had almost reached the other side, wavering on one stone while searching for another with none in suitable distance, when Captain Ward stepped forward and reached out his hand.

"I can manage," she told him, unwilling to accept his aid.

"I daresay, but I am less interested in your ability than in the length of time we are kept waiting while you are afraid to get your feet wet."

Hands closed around her waist and she was lifted bodily through the air and deposited on dry ground with scant respect for her dignity. Glaring at the Redcoat's back as he impatiently waved on the remaining troopers, Anstey smoothed her ruffled clothes and ignored the knowing grins from the watching soldiers.

Pointedly turning her shoulder, she remounted her horse and seated in the saddle ostentatiously gave her attention to the surrounding views; not even to herself

would she acknowledge that when James Ward had
lifted her, there had been one second of helplessness,
when she had felt something very like pleasure in his
nearness and strength. The emotion puzzled her and
she firmly refused to even contemplate it, turning her
mind instead to their journey and the miles that had
still to be covered.

CHAPTER
FIVE

PERPLEXED by her own emotions, her mind filled with uneasy thoughts, Anstey rode on, preoccupied and withdrawn. The headache and sore throat, that had vaguely bothered her for days, gradually became worse until by the time they reached Edinburgh, she could hardly lift her eyes for the pain that raged in her head.

She had never seen the capital, and a few months ago would have given much for the opportunity of visiting the city about which she had heard so much, but now she could raise no interest as they travelled along its narrow streets lined with tall grey stone buildings, dissected by dark mysterious openings leading into dim closes.

By morning she had developed a heavy cold with all its accompanying miseries, not least of which was the lack of a handkerchief to mop her streaming nose. Gazing down at the rows of close-built houses from the walls of the castle, she followed the line of the Long Mile with her eyes as it headed towards Holyrood Palace, and inevitably her mind was drawn towards the man who had caused her and her country so much heartache.

"What news of the Prince?" she found herself asking the Sergeant who happened to be standing by her while they waited for Captain Ward to arrive.

"The Pretender, you mean, miss?"

"I would hardly be enquiring after the Hanoverian usurpers," she answered with asperity. "I mean the rightful heir to the throne of Scotland – and England."

Sergeant Wright looked uneasy and shifted his weight unhappily from one foot to the other, but was saved from the necessity of answering by the presence of his superior officer, who had come up unnoticed.

"See to the men, Sergeant," said Captain Ward quietly and turned to Anstey. His broad shoulders shut her off from the milling soldiers, forming an illusion of privacy as he stared down at her, his eyes stern. "Have a care what you say, Miss Frazer," he warned. "Your rash unguarded tongue could lead you into trouble."

Anstey laughed scornfully. "More than I am already?" she wondered and suddenly irritated beyond measure by her uncomfortable symptoms, by the cold wind whipping up the hill and across the courtyard and most of all by the calm assurance of the man in front of her, she lashed out in anger, wanting to shake the Englishman's cool arrogance.

"Do you know what we call the Butcher Cumberland?" she asked, her voice pitched loud enough to carry to the ears of the nearby soldiers. "There's a pretty flower that has a strong perfume which you English call Sweet William – well, *we* call it Stinking Billy in his honour."

James Ward's lip curled. "What an exceedingly silly female you are," he remarked, not attempting to hide the contempt he felt. "If I didn't know your nose was sore from lack of a handkerchief, that your head was fit to burst and that you were chilled to the bone . . . *if* in fact I was not an understanding English gentleman, willing to make allowances for the infantile wiles of a stupid woman, you would be feeling the Sergeant's belt across your back even now. As it is, I'll pretend I haven't heard your childish outburst – and make you a present of my linen square."

Anstey accepted his handkerchief ungratefully, glowering after his upright back as he walked away, barely restraining herself from the luxury of stamping her foot.

"You was asking after the Stuart prince," said Sergeant Wright at her elbow, speaking quietly for her ears alone. "He's still free – in spite of the reward that's being offered."

"No one will betray him," she said, her eyes shining with pride. "However much is offered, no Scot will give him up to you."

The Sergeant shrugged. "We'll see," he said. "It's a lot of money, and I've seen for myself how poor some of your countrymen are."

"Poor but loyal," she told him fiercely.

"Daft some'ud call it. What's it matter who's king as long as there's a roof over your head and your belly's full?" He began to urge her towards the horses.

Anstey stopped in her tracks. "Sergeant!" she exclaimed shocked. "Have you no soul? No sensibility? No – *loyalty*?"

Will Wright was amused and showed it. "I follow whoever pays my wages," he said. "Only rich folk can afford loyalty."

This materialistic point of view occupied Anstey's

mind for most of the morning; living as she had in the Highlands where the clan system was still in operation and loyalty to one's chief an inborn factor of life, she found the Sergeant's outlook both unexpected and surprising. So busy was she with this intriguing concept that she gave little attention to the road along which she was riding, and when her mount put his hoof on a loose stone she was taken unawares and before she could recover, was pitched over his shoulder into a swirling, velvet darkness.

Surfacing briefly, she found herself wrapped in a cloak lying in the Sergeant's arms, and wondered at the concern in his face as he looked down at her, before slipping back into unconsciousness. The next time she awoke Anstey found herself in a strange bed, late afternoon sun streaming across the patchwork quilt that covered her. At her movement a girl rose from the window seat and smiling reassuringly left the room.

Anstey gazed about her, taking in the whitewashed walls and low ceiling crossed by old, dark beams. Sounds of people and animals drifted in at the open window, soothing in their normality after the vivid nightmares that had occupied her brain so recently.

The door opened and a motherly woman entered. "How are you feeling, my dear?" she asked.

Wrinkling her brow, Anstey frowned. "I have a headache," she said, and was surprised by the weakness of her voice.

"That's only to be expected, after that nasty knock you gave it. The doctor left a soothing draught for you to take when you awoke."

Obediently Anstey drank the bitter liquid. "Where

am I?" she asked, sinking back against the pillows.

"Why, at the Sour Plum in Galashiels to be sure –
the best inn in the town, though I say it myself. I'm
Molly Barton, the landlady."

"Have I been here long?"

"Four days, and you in a fever when the soldiers
brought you in. Muttering, you were, as the Captain
carried you in."

Anstey's heart stopped beating. "What was I saying?" she asked, one hand at her throat.

"Now then, there's no need for you to take on. I'm
sure a nice young man like Captain Ward wouldn't
listen to your secrets." She looked at the girl's face,
white and frightened above the counterpane, and took
pity on her anxiety. "You weren't saying anything to
worry about . . . something about Isabel, I heard and
you begging her not to do something."

After she had gone Anstey lay against her pillows
and wondered what she had said and how much of her
secret James Ward had gathered from her ramblings.
By evening she had fretted herself into a slight fever
again, wondering if she had let fall the fact that her
brother had fired the shot that had killed the English
officer, when he had come home to find Isabel struggling in his arms, and earned herself a scold from the
forthright landlady.

"What are you worrying about?" she asked. "I
thought you were on the mend, but if you're not
careful you'll be ill again. It's something to do with the
Captain, isn't it?" she went on shrewdly. "Shall I ask
him in – I wouldn't usually have a man in a young
lady's bedchamber but in the circumstances—"

Anstey shook her head, making the room swim, and

closed her eyes against the alarming sight. "I'm sorry to be a bother. . . ." Weak tears slid under her eyelids and rolled down her cheeks.

The landlady patted her shoulder. "Tired, that's what you are. You have a good sleep and you'll feel better in the morning."

Which in part was true; when Anstey awoke her head was clear and the dreadful weakness of the day before was gone, but the worry still filled her mind, nagging at her thoughts to the exclusion of all else as, wrapped in a borrowed shawl, she sat by the window and gazed at the busy street below with unseeing eyes.

The next afternoon Molly Barton appeared carrying a blue brocade dress over her arm. "You'll feel better dressed properly," she said briskly. "I told the Captain that I didn't hold with young ladies wearing breeches in my house and sent over to the seamstress for a gown which I happened to know had been ordered and not collected. . . . I took the liberty of buying a few other things I knew you'd need."

Anstey gazed at the pink stays and linen petticoats with real pleasure. "Didn't he mind?" she wondered.

The landlady snorted. "Didn't have the opportunity," she said. "Now come along and I'll help you to dress, and you'll feel more yourself."

After the time spent in masculine attire, Anstey found that to have her ribs encased again in tight, boned corsets was not a total pleasure, though the feel of skirts about her legs and the sight of herself in a becoming gown was very pleasant. Mrs. Barton even managed to gather up her short locks into a knot on top of her head and fasten them there with a length of blue ribbon.

"There," she said, eyeing her handiwork with approval. "No one'ud think you the same bedraggled little waif they carried in a few days ago. You look a proper pretty young lady. Just wait until that nice young Captain sets eyes on you."

Anstey looked at the older woman reflectively. "Mrs. Barton," she asked quietly, "what do you suppose my relationship to Captain Ward to be?"

"Why – I suppose he's escorting you to your family, I daresay your papa is another army officer."

Slowly Anstey shook her head. "I wish that was so," she said regretfully, "but in fact I am his prisoner. I am being taken to London, where I shall stand trial for – for killing an English officer when he came to my house."

Mrs. Barton sat down hastily on a convenient chair. "Well, I never did!" she gasped and stared at Anstey, the bright colour gone from her cheeks. "I won't ask you the whys and wherefores," she said at last. "It's none of my business . . . but I will say this: if you did so, I daresay there was a good reason. I've heard tales about the army's behaviour since Culloden."

"Oh, no, it was nothing like that," cried Anstey impulsively, "Captain Smythe was – it was all a terrible misunderstanding."

Molly Barton stood up briskly shaking out the folds of her skirt. "This Isabel you were talking about in your fever, what had she to do with it?" she asked shrewdly, to the other's dismay.

"Nothing – she had nothing to do with it at all. *Please* don't ask me any more." Trembling, Anstey turned away and to hide her nervousness peered at her reflection in the looking-glass, touching her hair and the lace at her shoulders with shaking fingers. "I haven't thanked you for my dress," she said, "and for your help."

"The Captain has ordered dinner for two in the parlour downstairs," announced Molly Barton.

"Oh, I couldn't – really, I—"

"About seven, he said." The landlady paused in the doorway, surveying the girl critically. "It'ud do you good," she observed.

Once alone, Anstey fell to wondering anxiously how much she had given away to the English soldier, nibbling her lips with anxiety as she waited for the expected summons and starting nervously to her feet when at last fingers tapped at her door.

"M-my compliments to Captain Ward," she called, "but I have the headache and will dine in my chamber."

"May I come in?"

Before she could reply the door was opened and James Ward entered. Wondering if he was aware of the beating of her heart which was shaking her, she stared at him.

"Mrs. Barton assures me that you are better, and that being so I wish you to dine with me – that we may discuss the future travel arrangements."

Bowing, he bent his elbow and proffered his arm to Anstey. Reluctantly she laid her hand on his sleeve and allowed him to lead her from the room, trying to hide the dread she felt of the forthcoming interview.

Like the rest of the inn, the parlour was a bright cosy room, low-beamed and panelled in dark wood.

Molly Barton herself served the meal, hurrying in with laden trays and a succession of succulent dishes

which she set before them with as much aplomb as if
she had been the finest chef in the kingdom. Anstey
kept up a flow of brittle chatter, afraid of any silence
which would give the Redcoat opposite the opportunity to mention her sister. At last the cheese and
wine was set on the table and the landlady, her duties
done, was forced to retire and leave them alone.

"Do you know why this inn has such an intriguing
name?" asked Anstey as the door closed behind the
ample form. "Mrs. Barton told me."

"I believe it's due to some English raiders being
caught robbing a plum tree," James Ward supplied
coolly.

Catching his eye, Anstey subsided, clasping her
hands together in her lap to still their tremor. For a
moment there was silence in the room and she stole a
glance at the soldier, finding him apparently studying
the depths of his wine as he twirled the glass between
his fingers. At last he spoke, making her start.

"Since we are so near England, I have decided that
you may wear female dress." He looked at her suddenly, a hint of a smile in his grey eyes. "I may say that
Mrs. Molly has been at pains to point out the moral
outrage of forcing a young lady to display her legs in
breeches. Bearing that in mind and your recent ill-
ness, I think it best for you to continue the journey in a
coach."

Anstey looked at him, while her heart slowed its
frantic beat and gradually returned to normal. So he
was not going to mention her delirious mutterings.
Hope began to rise in her breast and she sat up straight
in her chair.

"All being well, we will set out the day after tomorrow. Do you think you will be recovered by then?"

"Oh, yes," she cried brightly, her relief making her speak too forcefully and realizing her mistake she tried hastily to cover it with an explanation. "That is – I would that this journey was at an end. I grow tired of ceaseless travel."

"I am sorry to have put you to so much discomfort. I have not always been . . . kind, and for that I apologise."

Anstey stared across the table in astonishment. For the first time in their acquaintance there had been genuine warmth in his voice. Unable to think of anything to say, she sat in silence and after a while Captain Ward cleared his throat and reached across to refill her glass.

"After you fell the other day and while you were still unconscious you said a great deal in your delirium," he said, hesitating a little over his words. "Enough to make me realize that you were not responsible for Leo Smythe's unfortunate death."

Suddenly Anstey's hand, which had been in the act of reaching for her glass and had paused at his first word, was covered by strong, brown fingers. Wordlessly she gazed down at his hand emerging from the red uniform sleeve, while her breath quickened and her neckerchief rose and fell with her growing agitation.

"I will not deny that at first I regarded you with very real dislike, supposing you a murderess, but over the weeks we have been together I have felt a growing admiration for the staunchness of spirit with which you have met adversity. I have even come to respect the loyalty which you give to your cause, however mistaken." He leaned forward and holding her gaze spoke with grave intensity. "Confide in me, Miss Frazer and I give you my word to do all I can to see that the accusations against you are removed and the rightful criminal brought to justice."

Snatching away her hand, Anstey regarded him with horror, and suddenly knew what she must do unless all the sacrifices she had made so far were to be in vain and Isabel and Jamie still in danger.

"Let me help you. I would make amends for my treatment of you, and to that end I offer you . . . my friendship."

Anstey had the feeling that Captain Ward was offering very much more, and reluctantly closed her mind to her own response, regretting what she was forced to destroy.

"Friendship, sir!" she cried, making her voice ring with scorn. "Do you think I would accept friendship from a Redcoat? I want nothing, Captain Ward, from you or any other of your race."

James Ward sat back, his face hard, and already she could see the tentative kindness he had felt for her wither and die, and felt an unexpected grief at its passing.

"Forget whatever suspicions you are harbouring," she went on, searching for the unforgivable, "I shot your friend and my only wish is that it had been a hundred more of your English invaders."

"How very bloodthirsty. I vow you'd do credit to a melodrama. I've often heard tell that the female of the species is more deadly than the male, but until now I've not believed it." His eyes travelled disparagingly over her. "And you look such a delicate miss – so *petite* and womanly. One would not suppose that so pleasing an exterior hid so fierce a murderess."

Anstey flushed at his tone, but recalling her assumed role, lifted her chin. "Captain Smythe did not laugh," she told him, and at once wished the words unsaid.

The Englishman's grey eyes turned to ice, his mouth tightened and the skin across his cheekbones grew taut. The thin stem of the glass he had been holding snapped between his fingers, but he seemed totally unaware of the spots of blood that welled up like red raindrops.

Dear God, thought Anstey, *he's going to murder me*, and unable to tear her gaze away felt an icy shower of fear slide down her backbone.

Captain Ward looked down at his hand, and taking a handkerchief from his pocket twisted it around his fingers. He seemed to take an inordinate time over the simple task, but when he spoke again he appeared to have his emotions under control.

"Miss Frazer, you do yourself no good speaking in such a fashion," he said evenly. "However, I will accept your obvious dislike for the company of men of my race, and from now on you shall be treated with all the remoteness due to a prisoner of state." Standing up he bowed formally. "With your permission I shall withdraw. When you wish to retire you will find a trooper waiting to escort you to your room."

Without another glance he left the room, leaving Anstey to finish her wine, unhappily toying with her glass and aware, now that she had wantonly destroyed the tentative relationship the Englishman had offered, how much that fragile amity had come to mean to her.

From a bigoted dislike on both sides for that which the other represented, there had grown an unexpected respect, almost a guarded liking, and on her side at least a warmer feeling which she was reluctant to acknowledge.

She saw no more of Captain Ward until the morning of their departure from the Sour Plum, and then only fleetingly, for he acknowledged her presence with the briefest of nods and at once turned away to supervise the business of resuming the interrupted journey. Anstey surveyed the coach which had been hired with interest; in the Highlands travel was confined to horseback, but even to her eyes the vehicle appeared old and decrepit, its bodywork battered by countless journeys, while the wheels gave clear evidence of the many miles it had travelled since first it took to the road.

Reading her expression as he helped her into the dim interior, Sergeant Wright grinned. "Hardly fit for the Queen of Sheba," he commented, "but it's all we could find."

Closing the door, he climbed on to the driver's seat and gathered up the reins. Anstey looked about her at the torn leather seats and discoloured red lining. Her nose told her that sometime recently it had been used to transport onions, and while some efforts had obviously been made to clean the seats and remove the worst of the dirt, there still remained a general air of grime and disrepair which disgusted her. Wrinkling her nose with dislike, she drew her cloak carefully about her and reluctantly settled back against the ancient upholstery.

With a jolt and the promise of discomfort to come they set off. Anstey caught a glimpse of Molly Barton at an upstairs window, and leaned out of the coach to wave to her before a rut in the road threw her back in her seat with a jerk that jarred her teeth.

In the days that followed Anstey came to dislike that coach with a fervour that amounted to hatred. With unerring judgement it seemed to find every boulder and every unevenness in the road's surface, throwing her against the unpadded walls and across the hard seats until her body cried out in protest. Every muscle she owned ached, and she had long ceased to count her bruises which were so numerous that she appeared a variegated mass of purple and yellow.

Regardless of her discomfort, Captain Ward pressed on at top speed and having left Scotland behind they headed for Durham and the Great North Road with such haste that the Scottish girl was hardly aware that she had left her native country, and by the time she discovered the fact, she was so tired and weary that it seemed of little importance.

CHAPTER
SIX

THE days passed in monotonous regularity. At first
Anstey had been interested to see the tall verdant trees
and rich green pastures with their well-fed cattle, so
different to her own highlands with the few weather-
bent trees, and thin cows from which the poorer crof-
ters still took blood to mix with their porage in time of
need, but after a while the sight of such wealth palled
and she huddled back in her seat, hanging on to the
leather strap provided to protect herself from the
worst of the jolts and jars.

Once on the Great North Road the towns began to
pass in quicker succession, the sturdy stone houses of
Yorkshire seeming not unlike her native style of building to Anstey's Scottish eyes. Gradually the worst of
the violent motion grew less, and she realized that
either the roads were better or Sergeant Wright had at
last mastered the art of driving the four-horse team
that pulled the cumbersome vehicle.

Late one afternoon they drove into Thirsk, a quiet
market town with a new broad market-place and stopped at a new and prosperous inn. Here Anstey met
with the first dislike of her countrymen that she had
encountered; hearing her soft accent the landlord
demurred loudly at accepting the party, and only Captain Ward's looking down his thin nose and talking

about the King's business provided them with accommodation. As it was, Anstey's room was mean and dark with a single dormer window so high that her only view was of a neighbouring roof and a patch of sky. The sagging bed and rickety chair were so uninviting that she quit the squallid chamber as soon as she could, meaning to take refuge in the parlour, a more attractive apartment of which she had caught a glimpse as she climbed the stairs.

Entering somewhat hastily in case any should see her and send her back to her room, she closed the door and only then became aware that it was already occupied. A thin, drooping man in a snuff-coloured suit had been seated by the table and rose at her entrance.

For a second Anstey eyed him, taking an instant dislike to a certain shifty air about him as he bowed obsequiously to her.

"Madam, forgive me for troubling you. Our good landlord said someone would come, and I presume the gallant Captain is busy and has sent you in his stead. No doubt you are his lady wife?"

About to indignantly deny the unwelcome supposition, Anstey paused, wondering if it could be to her advantage to allow herself to be supposed the Englishman's spouse and instead of violently repudiating Captain Ward, seated herself and smiled graciously.

For a moment the man seemed uncertain how to begin, clearing his throat several times and running a finger around the inside of his none too clean cravat.

"Terrible times, madam," he said at last, his voice startlingly loud in the small parlour. As though surprised himself, he glanced uneasily at the door behind Anstey and threw a quick look over his shoulder at the window which gave on to the broad main street. "Terrible times we live in," he began again in carefully moderated tones, "with all that trouble up north and our brave fellows risking life and limb against the Scots – who are little better than savages, so I hear, living in mud huts and going about half naked."

Anstey's hands slowly clenched in her lap, but by now she had the man's measure, realizing clearly that he was about to divulge some information obviously damaging to the Jacobite cause. Concealing her feelings with difficulty, she waved him to a chair and intimated that she agreed with his estimation of her fellow-countrymen.

Thanking her profusely, he leaned forward with a confidential air. "You would not credit it, madam," he whispered, "but there are some who side with the rebels even here in Thirsk." He pursed his lips and nodded once or twice, watching her reaction with satisfaction, as Anstey managed to appear suitably shocked.

"There are some," he went on, "who wished for the Pretender to continue his march to London and who were dismayed when he lost the battle at Culloden, and even some who hope for his escape to France."

"You astonish me," Anstey told him, feeling some comment was called for.

He nodded again. "Traitors, I call them – that's why, as soon as I saw your husband's gallant troop ride in, I set about writing out a list."

"A – list?"

"The names of all the people who favour the Pretender." He produced a folded sheet of paper from his pocket and jumping to his feet, proffered it to Anstey.

Taking it reluctantly, she glanced distastefully at the columns of names. "Who are these people?" she wondered.

"Neighbours – tradesmen."

"And how did you hear these things? Surely they don't make their loyalties plain to all?"

"I keep a shop – I hear things."

"I see," said the girl slowly. "And does your shop do well?"

"Not so well as it did before Joss Bakewell set up next to me – and he's the worst of the lot. Only the other day I heard him say it was a shame to read in the newsheets about the treatment afforded the Scottish Rebels—"

Catching her eyes and reading the expression she was unable to conceal, he broke off and stared at her, his eyes narrowed. "I'll keep the list, madam, if you don't mind, and give it to your husband myself," he said, his hand stretched out to reclaim the paper she still held.

"What a weak female I am, to be sure, to feel sympathy for such wicked, wild men," Anstey cried hastily, eager to redress the mistake she had made. "My husband even tells me how soft-hearted I am. Why, only last week I wept a little when we saw a group of Scots hanged at Edinburgh. . . . You must make allowances for us frail womenfolk, but you would not like us so much were we not the soft, gentle creatures we are."

For a moment she thought she had gone too far, but the man's intelligence was as limited as she had supposed, and his expression cleared as an indulgent smile appeared on his thin face.

"The folk who fight against our good King George don't deserve a tear in your pretty eye," he said unctuously, and would have said more, but Anstey stood up and perforce he had to do the same.

"Be sure I will hand your list to my husband as soon as I see him," she said. "No doubt you will have thanks in the future for your good services to the King."

Well pleased, the man bowed himself out of the room. As soon as the door was closed behind him, Anstey smoothed out the folded paper and glanced at it again with a troubled gaze. Even while her eyes travelled down the column of ill-written names she heard Captain Ward's voice in the passage as he spoke to the landlord, and she barely had time to conceal the paper down the front of her bodice before the door was thrust open and the Redcoat officer entered.

Kicking the door to behind him, he folded his arms, and leaned his broad shoulders against it, eyeing her ominously. "The landlord tells me you had a visitor," he said.

Anstey took a deep breath. "H-hardly a visitor," she said lightly, casually putting the table between herself and the soldier. "There *was* a little man here, but he left—"

"He had something for me."

"Indeed? He must have grown tired of waiting. I daresay the landlord knows his name."

"The fellow's as new as his inn!" Janes Ward exclaimed, and Anstey's heart gave a throb of relief at the knowledge that the snuff-suited man would be difficult to find. "But he's certain the man had something he wished to give to me. The landlord says he left with a well-satisfied air – hardly the manner of a man frustrated in his wishes. Which must mean, my dear Miss Frazer, that he had carried out his desires . . . or thinks he had."

Lifting her shoulders delicately, Anstey smiled with assumed indifference, hoping that the man opposite would not detect her quickened breathing. "Perhaps he saw one of the servants, or a trooper," she suggested.

Captain Ward shook his head and at last lifted his shoulders away from the door. "No one save you," he told her baldly and advanced into the room.

Anstey forced a laugh. "You can hardly suppose he would hear my accent and give me anything intended for you."

"As you must know, your accent is of the lightest and with a little effort on your part, could be unnoticeable."

While he spoke, the Redcoat continued his slow progress towards her and against her will Anstey found herself backing away until she was trapped in the space between the low-burning fire and a large wooden settle.

"Where is it, Miss Frazer?" asked the soldier inexorably.

"Wh-what?" she asked in puzzled innocence.

"The folded paper the man showed the landlord before he came in here."

"Oh," she sighed and lowered her head to hide the dismay she felt from the penetrating gaze directed against her.

"Precisely. Pray give it to me and let there be an end to this foolishness." He waited for her to reply, but as she merely hung her head and remained silent he grew impatient. "I would remind you that my patience is not unlimited."

A shiver at the quiet menace in his voice shook Anstey, but she gathered her courage together and faced him bravely. "I cannot give it to you – I destroyed it."

"Liar," the man said pleasantly, for all there was a tight knot of anger at the corner of his mouth. "You had no time."

"The fire—"

"There is no burnt paper there. No, Miss Frazer, you have not destroyed the paper, but hidden it."

His eyes ran slowly and insolently over her, stopping at the neckline of her bodice and lingering there. Instinctively she covered it with her hand and a smile of satisfaction appeared on the soldier's face.

"I thought so," he said quietly. "It would take an ingenious woman to try another hiding place. Now, ma'am, shall you give it to me, or do you wish for the excitement of my hands upon your person?"

A vivid flush flared in Anstey's cheeks and heedless of the folly of her action, her hand flew up and struck at the smiling face above her with all her strength. Her wrist was seized and held in a merciless grip and while she cried in pain at the strength in the Redcoat's grasp, fingers delved between her breasts and the hidden paper was retrieved and thrust deep into Captain Ward's pocket.

"How dare you – oh, how dare you!" she breathed over a sob of rage and indignation.

"Very easily," she was told, and deliberately his brown hand slid again from her shoulder to the lace that edged her bodice.

Anstey cringed at his touch, tears of impotent anger running down her cheeks. Quickly she bent her head and sank her teeth into the wrist of the man who held her.

She was shaken off much as a terrier deals with a rat, and thrown roughly on to the settle to land in an undignified heap of petticoats.

"Stay there," commanded Captain Ward grimly standing over her, his expression hard and cold. Reading the threat in his eyes, Anstey subsided and lay still, watching as he took the paper from his pocket and perused it quickly, a frown between his eyebrows.

At last he looked up, raising his brows interrogatively. "Do you know what is here?"

Brushing aside the tears on her cheek with a hand that trembled, she sat up and nodded her head.

"A list of supposed Jacobites."

Quick to hear the note of scorn in his voice, she looked up, her eyes wide, in time to see the paper dropped into the embers of the fire and crushed among the coals by a booted foot. Wordlessly she gazed up at him, her mouth parted with astonishment.

"*Why?* Why did you do that?" she demanded.

His expression did not soften. "I've enough to do without taking part in a witch-hunt. Obviously the man is out for retribution over some hurt. I'll not lend my uniform to vindictive troublemaking."

Anstey sighed. "For a moment I thought you might have grown kinder towards the Hanoverians' opponents."

"Then, Miss Frazer, you thought wrong," was the uncompromising reply, and reaching down he took her arm and jerked her to her feet, holding her so close that she was forced to stretch her neck uncomfortably to meet his gaze. "I no more like the Jacobites than you care for the King's men, but one thing I will have plain."

He bent his head until his breath fanned her cheek, and said, his voice filled with quiet menace, "I grow tired of your behaviour, girl. With repetition, it becomes tedious – bore me again and I'll replace the bracelets you wore and enforce greater security of your person. No doubt you think yourself hard-done-by and ill-treated, but believe me I could make your life so miserable that you would regard your arrival in London with relief."

Anstey tried to lift her arm free of his grip, but his fingers tightened cruelly as he gave her an impatient shake. "I grow tired of your company, Miss Frazer," the Redcoat went on. "From now on you will have little time to embroil yourself in schemes or escapades. I intend to be in London in a week's time." He smiled thinly at the quick glance of dismay she sent him. "I see you realize the haste with which we shall travel. We'll journey late and set off early. They tell me the stage takes twelve days to reach Edinburgh from London – I have every intention of bettering that time."

During the next few days, Anstey had every cause to realize that Captain Ward intended to keep his word. Towns and villages seemed to fly by, and she came to know that any request for rest would fall upon deaf ears as the cavalcade hurried along the Great North

Road towards the capital of England. With every day the aged coach seemed to become more dilapidated and worn; the door was held closed with an improvised strap, a hole that appeared in the flooring was covered over with a square of wood. Altogether, the ancient vehicle gave every sign of being in the process of disintegration, and the fear of an accident was added to Anstey's already worried and weary brain as they drove deep into the heart of England.

Her fears were justified as they entered Lincolnshire, and the flat road and landscape spurred Sergeant Wright to greater speed. A few miles before they reached Grantham, there was an ominous crack and the coach lurched wildly as the spokes of one wheel snapped, the axle was driven into the ground and the whole equipage plunged over at an angle amid the screaming of frightened horses and the shouts of men.

Anstey found herself in a heap in the corner of the coach, dazed and bruised but otherwise unhurt. The door above her was opened and hands reached in to drag her to safety. Swiftly she was set on her feet, and after a cursory enquiry to her hurts was put into the care of a soldier, while the company's attention was turned to Sergeant Wright, who had been flung from the driving seat and lay still and pale with an already livid bruise rising on his forehead.

Under his fellows' rough but competent ministerings, he soon stirred and sat up, but seemed dazed and giddy, complaining in no uncertain manner of the headache that troubled him.

The accident had taken place near a substantial farmhouse, the owner of which now approached and offered his services.

"My good wife has ale enough for your lads," he said, "and wine for yourself, sir, put ready in the parlour by my daughters. I've even a wright as can give a hand to that wheel for you."

"My thanks, farmer, and we'd all be grateful for your hospitality," returned the officer, "but that wheel is beyond repair if I mistake it not."

"My man can make a good job of it," said the farmer sturdily. "We has to be good with our hands, if we're not to send into Grantham every time anything goes wrong."

The Redcoat smiled. "I'd be grateful, then, and even more so if you'd take my Sergeant and the lady we're escorting into the care of your house."

"Escorting?" Shrewd eyes turned in Anstey's direction. "Why be that, then?" he asked baldly.

"The lady is a Jacobite," he was told curtly.

"Then she'll have none of my hospitality. I've had enough of them Jacobites – affrightening my females into hysterics and putting the country into a turmoil. The price of wheat'll go down, you mark my words."

"I'm sure you are right," Captain Ward agreed wearily, "but the prisoner cannot stay here while the coach is repaired. She is not so desperate a criminal that you need feel endangered by her presence under your roof."

The farmer considered. "W – ell, I daresay there's an outhouse as will take her," he said at last, "but I'll not be responsible if she gets away, mind."

Anstey, who had listened to this exchange in stony-faced silence, lifted her chin and stared disdainfully down her nose at the older man.

"I'll give you my word, Captain, not to escape," she said, "I have no wish to test this fellow's outbuildings."

"I thought they all spoke some mumbo-jumbo o' their own," the farmer exclaimed. "Sounds English, she does."

Drawing herself up to her full height, Anstey took a deep breath. "I am a Scot," she told him proudly. "My ancestors were civilized when yours cowered in caves."

The farmer blinked under this unexpected attack, but the officer, growing impatient, sent the Sergeant and Anstey under the care of two soldiers to the confines of the farm and turned himself to the business of repairing the damaged coach.

Afterwards, Anstey could only suppose that some impulse made her pluck one of the farmer's white roses as they passed through his garden and deliberately tuck it into the bodice of her dress. Seeing her action, as she had intended, he rumbled his annoyance and grew red in the face.

"Why, farmer," she said sweetly, "I'd almost question your loyalty – having a whole bushful of Jacobite favours in your garden. You must know that the white rose is the Prince's symbol."

His colour grew alarming and she wondered if he would have an apoplexy, but although he was forced to mop his face vigorously, he controlled his emotions while he pushed her into a small stone building and barred the stout door, his heavy footsteps as he stamped away indicative of his feelings.

The hours passed slowly for Anstey, who had soon explored the narrow confines of her prison and had quickly come to the realization that there would be no escape for her from the strange little building. Showing signs of having been recently whitewashed, it contained nothing save herself, and she was forced to sit on the floor while the sun rose higher and the interior became hot and airless. Some time later, when the pangs of both thirst and hunger had made themselves felt, she heard voices and movement in the yard outside and raised her heavy head from her knees as the door was opened.

Eager for release, she scrambled to her feet but the brilliant sunlight after the darkness of her prison blinded her and suddenly her head began to spin. Stumbling against the wall, she would have fallen had hands not supported her. For a moment all was darkness and then she felt blessed coolness on her face and water was held to her lips.

"This was inhuman," she heard Captain Ward say, and opened her eyes to find him regarding the sullen farmer with obvious anger.

"Your men should have cared for her," the man defended himself. "Besides, I had to ride into Grantham."

"If you've made our arrival known, I shall make it my business to see that you are punished," James Ward told him, his voice tight with annoyance. He had chosen to ignore the charge against his troopers, but the glance he flung in their direction promised much and made them shift their feet uneasily.

Without further ado, he gave curt orders for the men to mount and hauled Anstey to her feet. She had thought his anger for the farmer alone, but now saw that a great part of his annoyance was reserved for her.

THE REBEL AND THE REDCOAT   99

The limp rose was snatched from her bosom with scant regard for the delicate lace in which it was entangled or for the thorns that barbed its long stem. Heedless of the red drops that appeared on the girl's pale skin, he tossed aside the Prince's favour and glared at her.

"You are extremely foolish, Miss Frazer," he told her, his lip curling contemptuously. "Now all the town will be waiting for you . . . and I've an idea that your reception will not be to your liking. From the farmer's reaction, you should have realized that Jacobites are held in little liking in these parts. Derby is not far away, and the Pretender's arrival there must have filled the local people with alarm. Methinks you'll find that they regard you as a target for their anger at the fears they felt."

The Redcoat's supposition was proved right when they were met on the outskirts of Grantham by a group of people, obviously waiting for the coach. Shouts and jeers followed them as they passed, and the people who turned and ran after the column were quickly joined by more, until by the time Anstey and the soldiers reached the centre of the town they were surrounded by a large, hostile crowd. Following their officer's orders, the troopers closed up protectively around the coach and its occupant, but even so, Anstey was far from safe.

At first she had sat upright and tried to ignore the threatening faces outside, but soon gestures were followed by missiles and a volley of stones struck the coach and the escorting horses, who were already nervous at the atmosphere, making them sweat and shy nervously.

Sergeant Wright had recovered enough to insist upon his ability to drive the coach and horses and now he brought the equipage to a halt outside the Angel, Grantham's oldest hostelry. Seizing the moment, the crowd surged forward and broke through the cordon of soldiers to beat upon the vehicle's ancient sides. While some attempted to open the door, others shook it so violently that it was in danger of turning over for the second time that day, and Anstey, more terrified than she thought possible, could only attempt to elude the clutching hands and pray for the horrific moment to end.

Suddenly she became aware of a new movement outside, and the threatening growl of the crowd gradually grew silent, as the people first were still and then began to withdraw from the coach into a protective, anonymous throng. Following their retreat, Anstey turned her head and saw a group of soldiers standing on the steps of the inn, their muskets cocked and every line of their figures bespeaking grim determination as they faced their fellow-countrymen with loaded weapons.

Captain Ward stared about him, his eyes glittering in his pale face. "I have in my custody the King's prisoner," he told the uneasy men and women, "and I intend to take her safely to London."

"Hang the wench here," shouted a voice from the crowd and several others took up the cry.

"In England no one is hanged without a trial," they were told. "If you would see the rebels punished then you must come to London – I'm willing to take the foremost among you there as my prisoners."

Someone laughed at his sally, and taking advantage

as the mood of the mob lightened, the Redcoat ordered two troopers to escort the prisoner from the coach into the inn. At sight of her the rabble pressed forward again, jostling the surrounding soldiers in their eagerness to catch a glimpse of the Jacobite rebel in their midst. A few of the braver set up a jeering catcall, but mindful of the silent, watchful soldiers on the steps of the Angel, nothing more was attempted, though the closed, angry faces told plainly that their mood was dangerous, only the presence of the armed Redcoats restraining them from violent action.

As Anstey was hurried up the steps a stone was hurled from the depths of the crowd, and as though at a signal the mob surged forward again, people at the rear pressing against their fellows in the fore who were thrown willy-nilly against the mounted troopers, and for a moment all was confusion as men fought and shouted, soldiers laid about them with the flats of their swords, and the coach horses, tried beyond endurance and Sergeant Wright's capabilities, reared and plunged, clearing a way through the mob as they set off at an untidy gallop.

Anstey's arm was seized and she was dragged into the interior of the inn and the door hastily closed and barred behind her.

"She can't stay here, sir – she can't stay here," the landlord said, his voice high and his jowls aquiver with fright. "They'll tear my inn to pieces."

"Not with my men outside," Captain Ward told him curtly, "but I've no intention of staying here. I take it you have a back way – then saddle me a horse and I'll not trouble you further."

He looked down at Anstey, whose arm he still held,

and became aware for the first time that she was trembling in his grasp. "Don't be afraid – they shan't get you," he said roughly.

Lifting her head, she gave a half-sob, half-laugh and pushed her loosened hair back from her face, revealing a bruise high on one cheekbone and a trickle of blood where a stone from the rabble had found its target. "P-perhaps they – don't care for the journey to London to see me dance," she said breathlessly, and slipped through his hands as she slid limply to the floor.

Captain Ward cursed under his breath before bending to lift her into his arms, he turned to give hurried instructions to the soldier who had followed him into the inn.

"Allow some time to elapse after I am gone," he said, "then make the landlord announce that we are no longer here. Once the mob is satisfied on that score I hope they will disperse. As soon as that happens, the troop is to remove itself from Grantham with all speed. Take the Great North Road south and follow it for some ten miles to a crossroads with a great oak, take the left fork until you come upon a pair of gates surmounted by an eagle, which is the entrance to my house. With luck I should already be there."

Tossing Anstey higher against his shoulder, he paused only long enough to be sure that his orders were understood, then strode quickly away as another volley of stones spent itself against the sturdy oak door behind him.

Anstey slowly became aware of cool evening air blowing against her, of an uneven motion under her and of

being held by a strong arm. The previous events
returned in all their terrifying vividness and she lifted
her cheek from the red coat against which it rested
with a cry of fear, straining against the arm that held
her.

"Quietly – quietly," soothed James Ward, as his
grip tightened against her struggles and for a moment
he checked his mount's speed. "You're safe. We're
clear away, with no one following."

Taking in his words, the girl allowed herself to relax
against him, her cheek returning to its former position
against his bright red coat. For a moment she enjoyed
the rush of cool air and the feeling of security after
danger that the firm grip around her brought, before
recalling whose arm it was that held her so comfortingly. She moved and sat up, withdrawing from the
close proximity in which she found herself.

At once his grasp slackened and Anstey found herself forced to catch at the pommel of the saddle for
support as the animal beneath her galloped on, heedless of the double burden he carried.

For a while she was allowed to bounce around
uncomfortably before Captain Ward's arm returned
to her waist and she was drawn back against his chest.
"Much better to forget who I am," he said against her
ear. "Pretend I'm a bonny Highlander, if you must,
but don't spurn my arm, I pray."

"Where are you taking me?" she demanded, having
been silent for several minutes.

"To Wrexford Manor."

Anstey digested this in silence. "I daresay you have
a reason," she observed at last, "but I would like to
hear it."

His arm tightened about her waist. "It happens to be my home," he told her, feeling her stiffen as she took in his words, "and seems as good a place as any in which to spend the night."

CHAPTER
SEVEN

Dusk had begun to fall when they reached the gates of Wrexford Manor, but even in the grey light and tired as she was, Anstey lifted her head to stare at the house as they approached it; to her Highland eyes it appeared totally unlike any she had known. In her homeland houses were built of mud and turf like the rude crofts of the poor folk, or of stone and fortified; nowhere would a house of red brick be found. With its rosy walls and white cornices and window-frames, Wrexford Manor seemed to her strange and oddly unsubstantial.

The door was opened at their approach and an old man bowed as Captain Ward slid from the horse and lifted Anstey down. Apparently feeling her incapable of negotiating the shallow steps and doorway, he carried her into the hall, swinging round as two women appeared.

"James!" the elder cried joyfully at sight of him, her gladness only diminishing slightly at the girl in his arms. "And . . . a friend. How delightful."

Anstey was deposited on her feet, but the soldier retained a tight grip on her wrist as he smiled at the ladies.

"Mama," he said, kissing her hand. "How good it is to see you." He turned to the other, whom Anstey could now see was very young, scarce out of the schoolroom, she judged by her fresh countenance. "And Caro – no kiss for your big brother?"

"The lady, James," reminded his mother gently. "Introduce us, pray."

"This is Miss Anstey Frazer of Glentyre in Scotland." As curtseys were exchanged he went on, "I am afraid that she is no ordinary guest, but a rebel whom I am escorting to London for trial. I would not have brought her here, but we were met at Grantham by a mob intent upon mischief and for her safety, I had to ride ahead leaving my troop to follow." He smiled suddenly, looking fondly at his mother. "I hope your store cupboard is well stocked – I left word at the gate to let them in. They should be here before night."

"James!" ejaculated his mother faintly. "A whole troop! Where will they sleep?"

"The stables will do for a night – which reminds me. Miss Frazer can have the green bedroom. Will you give orders to have it made ready?"

"The Green Room?" put in his sister, who had been eyeing Anstey with curiosity. "Why, James, it's at the side and the windows stick."

"Precisely," agreed James Ward. "I chose it for that very reason. Miss Frazer has a propensity for escape, and unless I am to tie her hand and foot or set a guard to watch her, the Green Room is the very thing."

Caroline's eyes grew large at the implication behind his words and for the first time the two English women took in the other's dishevelled appearance.

"The child's fit to drop," exclaimed Mrs. Ward suddenly, "and is hurt into the bargain."

Anstey found herself the object of the Redcoat's cool survey. His expression softened a little as he observed how pale she was and how shadowed her eyes. Tilting her chin, he touched the bruise and tiny cut on her cheekbone with one finger, probing gently. "Your beauty will survive," he told her ironically.

"Let me take her to my chamber to see to her comfort while the Green Room is seen to," suggested his mother.

"An you try to escape, you'll spend the night in the cellars," the soldier warned quietly, and pinched Anstey's chin warningly before releasing her.

Anstey allowed Mrs. Ward and her maid to minister to her, grateful for their kindness, but too weary to appreciate the bath and food, longing only for a bed and the bliss of falling asleep. She awoke to find brilliant sunshine streaming into her room, and now could enjoy the luxury of a clean body and fresh linen as she stretched sensually in the soft bed.

She was out of bed exploring the room, and had just discovered with some amusement that Captain Ward had been right about the windows, when footsteps sounded in the passage and after a brief tap, a key turned in the lock and the door opened to reveal Mrs. Ward's maid with a breakfast tray.

"Ring the bell when you're ready," she said, having settled Anstey with the tray across her lap, "and I'll come and dress you. Miss Caroline has put out a gown and linen. I took the liberty of washing your clothes, miss."

When she was alone, Anstey pulled a little face at the servant's disparaging tone, but later had to allow that Caroline Ward's clothes were more becoming than the ones Molly Barton had acquired for her all those days ago in Scotland. Admiring the cream-and-pink striped dress in the mirror, she slipped her hand into the pocket tied about her waist under the full skirt, and to her surprise her fingers closed upon something. Withdrawing her hand she found herself clutching a knot of white ribbon, and catching her breath, stared at it in amazement as she wondered who, among this Hanoverian household, could have sent her the Prince's favour, that Jacobite ladies wore in their hair to declare their loyalty. There seemed only one possible person, and when some time later Caroline slipped furtively into the room she was not surprised.

Finger to her lips, the girl cautioned her to silence with all the air of a great conspirator. "How I admire you," she whispered. "Did you find my signal that you were not totally alone? Even in England there are some still loyal to the Stuart's cause. I will do all in my power to aid you."

"Leave the door unlocked," Anstey suggested, practically.

"Well, that would serve very little; not only are we a long way from anywhere, so that you'd be caught before you could reach safety, but one of the footmen is sitting at the head of the stairs . . . but I have an idea. I won't tell you what it is, in case it doesn't work out, but be ready at a moment's notice, and when you least expect it."

Anstey smiled at the other's mysterious manner, reminded that Caroline had only recently left the schoolroom and still retained much of her childish brashness.

"I daresay James would lock me in my room if he found me here, but I am willing to face danger for my cause." She paused and looked at Anstey curiously. "Did he illtreat you?" she asked. "Mama asked him the same question, and he grew quite red and uneasy."

"He – was not always kind," Anstey replied reluctantly.

"He has been quite brutal with me – once he boxed my ears for riding a new horse he'd bought, so you see I can sympathise with you." Caroline leaned closer and whispered conspiratorially. "Tell me about the Prince. Have you met him?"

"I'm afraid he didn't come to my part of the world, but my father joined his forces and was at Culloden. He said he was a fine, handsome chevalier with the air of a king."

Caroline sighed with satisfaction. "Oh, how I *wish* I had been there," she cried. "I vow I would willingly die for him."

"Many did," Anstey told her soberly, shaking her head at the other's questioning glance. "No, my father got away and is now in France."

"Tell me why you are a prisoner. James sent me to bed while he told Mama."

"Then I feel he does not wish you to know."

"La! I'd have thought that a very good reason for you to tell me." Caroline giggled suddenly. "I listened at the door and heard most of the story. You killed a soldier who was attempting your honour."

Anstey looked down suddenly, realising that to the younger girl the whole episode, which was so painful to her, appeared a romantic fairytale.

"A soldier called Leo Smythe died, Caroline," she said. "He had a wife and a baby and now only the child is left. It was a sordid happening, and I would give much for it not to have happened."

The other girl grew sober and viewed her anxiously. "How foolish you must think me," she said slowly, "but truly I had not thought. It seemed like a play to me."

Anstey reached across to pat her hand. "Like you, until this happened I had little contact with the harsher side of life."

"What can I do for you?"

The serious note in Caroline's voice told the other that the dreams and fancies had faded and that now she was offering practical help.

"Ask leave for me to walk in the garden."

"If you truly wish to, I shall use my best wiles to your advantage." Eager to begin, Caroline jumped to her feet and hurried to the door pausing to add with a roguish smile, "James, you know, is not the ogre I painted him. He is really quite amiable. I shall have to be very clever and *suggest* your wish to him, for he must not know I have been here. Pray do not mention my visit to him – he has no idea that I am loyal to the Prince."

With a rustle of silk she was gone, leaving the Scots girl to smile a little at her youthful exuberance. She was doubtful of her prevailing upon Captain Ward's kindness, but about midday the door was opened and the maid bade her to follow. Pausing only to smile charmingly at the footman on the landing, Anstey followed her down the stairs and found the Redcoat officer waiting in the hall. He turned at the sound of her step and for a moment she met his gaze steadily before he came forward and offered her his hand down the last few stairs.

"My sister suggests that you might care for a walk in the garden."

"Indeed, I would," she returned warmly and he led her towards the open front door, retaining her hand and tucking it into the corner of his elbow.

For a while they walked in silence, the man deep in thought and the girl with eyes only for the garden; the luxuriant leaves and grass and the abundant blossoms filling her with wonder and envy.

At last she sighed. "If only we could grow such flowers in Scotland," she said softly.

James Ward looked down at her. "My father set them out," he told her. "It was his greatest joy. He could make anything grow and always said he inherited green fingers from his grandmother, who was Dutch and whose family left Holland and settled here in Lincolnshire, which is much like their country. They brought bulbs with them and grew rich on tulips."

"Tulips," she repeated. "I've heard of them and even stitched their shape on embroidery, but I've never seen the real flower."

"They stand like so many soldiers with red hats instead of black. In spring the garden is ablaze with them. You should come and see—"

Realizing the impossibility of what he had said, James Ward broke off abruptly, staring down at Anstey with a frown between his black brows.

"The spring is a long time away – and who knows where I shall be then?" the girl forced herself to say coolly, well aware of the thought that was in both their minds.

"This madness has gone far enough," said the Redcoat impatiently. "We both know full well that you did not shoot Leo Smythe. It's time you ceased protecting your sister and thought of yourself."

Anstey looked at him. "Isabel did not kill Lieutenant Smythe," she told him truthfully.

"No one would search Scotland for her – take my word for it."

"You Redcoats came for me – besides, she did not do it."

"Then say she did," he told her between his teeth. "What does the fate of one idiot girl matter?"

"She is my sister!"

"Sister or not, she does not weigh against you—"

"How can you say that? Oh, how *can* you? She is a dear, good person, kind and loving, too innocent to have the vices of us cleverer folk. Isabel is one who should be loved and cared for, and you would have me submit her to – this," she made a gesture, indicating her own captive state, "to what has happened to me. She would have no conception or understanding of what or why. Take her away from the Highlands and the life she knows, Captain Ward, and you'd have no need to employ a headsman. She'd pine away before she reached Edinburgh."

"And you, Miss Frazer? *You* did not pine away."

"I am of tougher stuff," Anstey told him simply.

"Your stupid stubbornness will be your own death warrant."

She faced him, her eyes wide as she met his. "Anyone would suppose you cared, Captain."

Giving an exasperated snort, he swung away a few paces, his boots crunching on the gravel path. "I care for a miscarriage of justice," he said harshly over his shoulder. "In this case, I am persuaded that you are innocent of Smythe's murder."

She gave a brittle, shaking laugh. "I find your concern touching, if misplaced. Whether I shot your friend or not, I am still a Jacobite, Captain Ward, and as such am an enemy of your country. As a true, loyal Englishman you should be thankful that I am captive and can do little to serve my Prince save involve a whole troop, who might be searching for him, in the business of escorting me to London. I am glad that I have kept you and your men away from the Highlands. Take my advice, Redcoat, and don't rest on your laurels until you have me safe in jail."

James Ward showed his teeth in a smile. "Vixen," he said and an unexpected note in his voice made Anstey catch her breath and take an involuntary step backwards. "Your fierceness doesn't deceive me—"

"I am loyal to Prince Charles. I am proud of my Jacobite politics. While I deplore the fact of Lieutenant Smythe's death, I have confessed to it and will not change my words."

Defeated for the moment, the Redcoat fell silent, shrugging indifferently as he turned away, but his thoughtful air caused Mrs. Ward to send him many questioning glances during the midday meal.

"James," she said at last, "what are you planning? Don't deny me, for I have known that withdrawn look of yours since you were in the nursery."

Looking up, he gave his mother a preoccupied smile and assured her that he was merely giving his thoughts to some trifling matter that plagued him.

"I wish you could have stayed longer," said Mrs. Ward, following her own train of thought, "but I must own to no little gladness that I did not, after all, have to play hostess to your troops. Such dreadful times we live in – who would have thought that they would have been detained by a mob in Grantham of all places?"

"I am afraid that feeling against the Jacobites runs high," he told her soberly. "If the Pretender had not reached Derby I daresay the local folk would have felt little involved in the Rebellion, but having him so near aroused their fears – they are unable to forgive their fright."

"She seems quite a nice girl," offered his mother tentatively, watching her son.

"Yes," he returned baldly and changed the conversation, reminding her that he intended to leave to rejoin his troop as soon as luncheon was over.

Becomingly attired in a riding habit bestowed on her by Caroline, Anstey took her leave of the two ladies, rather amused to find a slip of paper pressed into her hand by the younger one as she thanked them for their care. Seated in the saddle she glanced at the note under cover of pulling on her gloves and saw the enigmatic message 'Be ready' in sharp black writing embellished in one corner by a somewhat uncertain drawing of a rose. Looking up, she caught Caroline's eyes upon her and smiled, receiving a conspiratorial nod in return.

"I understand that the soldiers were delayed," Anstey said, breaking the silence as they rode out of the grounds of Wrexford Manor and headed towards the main road.

"We'll meet them at the crossroads," Captain Ward told her. "You have nothing to fear, this part of the countryside is peaceful and one of my men rode from Grantham last night and back again with my orders. The troop will be awaiting us at the crossroads and until then nothing can happen."

Anstey was not reassured, her spine prickling with presentment and the memory of Caroline's note, but she did her best to hide her unease, riding demurely at the Redcoat's side.

They were a few miles on their journey and had just ridden into a sunken part of the road over which tall trees entwined their branches and cut off the light, when several dark figures left their hiding places and rode down the slope.

Eyes narrowed, the soldier placed himself in front of the girl, his hand on the stock of the pistol in its holster by his knee as he waited the strangers' approach. As they rode nearer and her eyes grew accustomed to the dim light, Anstey caught her breath as she saw the black masks covering their faces. Apparently the Redcoat noticed them at the same time, for he suddenly drew the long horse pistol and cocked it threateningly.

"Hold!" he commanded.

For a second the masked men hesitated, then there was a loud report and a flash from higher up the bank where a fourth man had waited unobserved, and Captain Ward's weapon tumbled to the ground while the soldier himself clutched his shoulder with fingers that rapidly turned red, and swayed in the saddle.

Anstey watched horrified, the speed of events dulling her brain until her bridle was seized by one of the figures and she recovered her wits enough to fight for control of her horse.

"Mistress Frazer, Mistress Frazer, we are friends," the man said to her surprise. "We are Jacobites, here to help you to escape."

Wide-eyed, Anstey looked across at the face behind the mask, seeing its youth and examining the others in turn, realized that here was the result of Caroline Ward's mysterious behaviour.

"Come with us – there is no time to lose," urged the one who held her bridle and the others shifted in their saddles, glancing uneasily over their shoulders, obviously eager to be gone.

"The wench has lost her senses – don't argue with her. Lead her horse, or I will."

As he spoke, the man thrust a smoking pistol back into his pocket and realizing that he must have been the one to shoot the Redcoat, Anstey looked at him more carefully, noting the smooth chin and mouth that was tightly compressed to stop it quivering.

Ignoring his companion, the nearest rider gave her his attention. "You are quite safe – come with us, there is no time to spare. Caroline arranged this – she told us of you and we came to rescue you—"

Anstey stared at him, her face tense. "Did she arrange, also, for her brother to be shot?"

His face grew as pale as hers. "That was an accident," he told her, unhappily.

"And now you would leave him here, wounded and unattended? You are as bad as Butcher Cumberland."

He flinched at the scorn in her voice and as though to point her words, Captain Ward chose that moment to slide from his horse and lie limp and deathly white on the muddy ground. With an exclamation, Anstey slid from her saddle to kneel beside him, trying to staunch the blood with the linen cravat she dragged from her neck, her mind taken back momentarily to the time when she had tended Johnnie Gray.

"You had better go," she told the would-be rescuers, who were watching her silently. "The Captain's troop is on its way from Grantham. They may arrive at any moment."

"You must come! We came to save you. Stay here and you'll be taken to London to stand trial as a rebel," they told her, bewildered.

"I cannot leave him," she said simply, unable to explain her action even to herself.

"Then one of us will stay, if only you will go."

"Use your brains," she said curtly. "What use is it to sacrifice yourself for me? Think of the heartbreak for your family." She looked at them. "I'd lay wager that none of you are long out of the schoolroom. No, gentlemen, I appreciate your offer and am grateful for your brave act, but I shall stay here – *you* will go, and quickly."

She smiled up into their nonplussed faces, touched suddenly by their youth and bewildered dejection. "Go home, gentlemen," she said gently, "and forget this ever happened. For all Captain Ward knows, we were attacked by highwaymen."

Slowly, reluctantly, and with many backward glances, they went. Disdaining the road, they trotted up the bank, paused for a moment on the ridge as though hoping she would change her mind and let them play the heroic role they wished for, before they plunged over the skyline and vanished.

Once alone, Anstey renewed her attentions to the unconscious figure on the ground. The bleeding seemed to have stopped and she dared to disturb him while she felt in his pocket for the brandy flask she knew he carried. As she withdrew the silver container, the soldier groaned and stirred, opening his eyes to stare at her blankly.

With surprising speed his fingers closed over her hand in a grip that made her wince. "Would you rob the wounded?" he asked thickly and throwing her from him, scrambled to his knees.

From where she had fallen, the girl watched him and saw that the effort had been too much and that he leaned against a tree-trunk for support. Rising, she approached him cautiously, wondering if his senses had returned.

"James," she said softly, unaware that she used his first name, "James – it's me. Anstey Frazer."

She saw recognition in his eyes as he turned and looked at her, before he frowned and glanced about, his expression puzzled.

"Highwaymen," she supplied quickly, before he should give the matter too much thought. "We were attacked and you were shot – when I told them your troopers were on the way they rode off."

"They seem singularly cowardly . . . surely I recollect several of them? Which way did they go?"

Without thinking she indicated the opposite side of the road to the one her erstwhile rescuers had taken and knew at once how foolish she had been when she followed the soldier's eyes to the hoofmarks in the muddy ground, all clearly leading towards the other bank. Looking up she found the clear, grey gaze regarding her thoughtfully.

"Jacobites?" he asked quietly, holding out his hand for the flask.

Her nod was almost imperceptible.

"Why didn't you go with them?"

The question hung in the air, and unable to answer it she rose and went to the horses who were calmly cropping tufts of grass a short distance away. They took little notice of her approach and she was able to gather their dangling reins. Their velvet noses were warm and soft beneath her fingers, the sounds of them munching and their bits jingling, comfortingly familiar.

"Why, Miss Frazer?" asked a voice at her shoulder – she was turned gently to look up at the face above her.

James Ward had regained most of his colour and save for the ugly hole in his uniform, seemed little the worse for the adventure.

"Is that why you wear red coats?" she asked. "To hide the blood?"

Disregarding her question, he repeated his own. "Why didn't you make good your escape while you had the opportunity? No one would have found me for some time – you knew my troop is waiting at the crossroads."

"I told them that they were riding to join us, that's why they went." She laughed a little. "They were only children, and so determined to be heroes!"

"They could still have got you away. Why didn't you go with them?"

"I – found I could not," she answered very low.

He regarded her steadily, his head bent to hers. "In reality, I could not leave you wounded . . . and alone."

Turning away abruptly, he went in search of his pistol, returning it to the holster on his saddle before speaking again.

"This can make no difference," he said his voice harsh. "I still hold the King's commission. I still owe him my loyalty – no matter how much it costs me. I must still take you to London."

"I had not thought to influence you."

Her quiet voice hung in the air between them. The Englishman turned away with a muffled oath, and stared at the road with unseeing eyes.

"Your wound should be attended to," Anstey reminded him at last.

"I've had worse and stopped in the saddle."

She was surprised. "I thought you might return to your home."

"No. The sooner this business is over the better I shall be pleased. We'll ride for London with all speed, so mount up, Miss Frazer, and let us be on our way."

Understanding the divided emotions that made him speak harshly and well aware of her own warring feelings, Anstey obeyed him, sighing for what might have been with vague longings as she found a convenient boulder to serve as a mounting-block and climbed back into the saddle.

CHAPTER
EIGHT

WHEN they reached the crossroads and found the troop waiting for them, Anstey was glad to see that the decrepit old coach was nowhere in sight, and hoped fervently that it might have been abandoned. Sergeant Wright held the reins of a large horse with the virtuous air of a man wanting to convince others of the justness of his action, and snapped a smart salute as his officer approached.

"The coach, sir," he said. "I left it behind as a decoy – thought it might distract the mob, sir."

Captain Ward regarded him gravely, well aware of the battle between the ancient vehicle and the soldier which had assumed huge proportions as Will Wright fought for supremacy. "Good idea, Sergeant," he said. "I'm glad to see you none the worse for the fall you had."

The Sergeant grinned suddenly. "Almost think the blessed thing was alive at times – I swore it was trying to kill me. Fought me all the way from Scotland it did, throws me on me head and then if it don't run away with me! I can tell you, sir, I was *glad* to leave it behind, and I only hopes as they burn it when they find we've left."

"Never mind, Sergeant, you can always get a job as a coach-driver when you leave the army."

The Sergeant laughed. "Not me," he said. "I'm all set to own a nice little inn somewhere—" He broke off abruptly as he noticed the damp stain on Captain Ward's coat. His demeanour changed, sobered on the instant and he stepped forward quickly. "You're hurt—!" he began.

"A scratch – nothing to bother about," he was assured. "We had a skirmish with a pack of not very efficient highwaymen. Miss Frazer sent them flying with tales of your approach."

The Sergeant spared Anstey a shrewd glance, making her feel that he understood much more than was said. However, he appeared satisfied with the explanation, but the girl noticed that he was alert and wary as he rode, his hand never far from the butt of the big horse-pistol at his knee.

Forgetful of the fatigue she had felt on the former long ride, Anstey was glad to have exchanged the confines of the lumbering coach for the open air and the illusory freedom of a horse's back. The borrowed sapphire-coloured velvet riding habit was elegant and fashionable, its long trailing skirt moulding the lines of her legs before it fell away in graceful folds. With the little blue tricorne hat dipped becomingly over one eyebrow and the jacket cut in masculine lines, she felt like a dashing boy, the admiring glances thrown in her direction by the accompanying soldiers making her aware of how attractive she looked.

The bright sunshine of the morning gradually gave way to an overcast sky and by late afternoon rain had begun to fall in a steady manner that made it plain that it had set in for the rest of the day. Cursing his lack of foresight in not providing Anstey with a cloak, James Ward flung his own over her, and soon his brave red uniform was soaked and dull. The rain dripped out of his black tricorne, adding to his general discomfort. Despite his wish to continue the journey he looked about for shelter, at last spying a large barn beside the road to which he led his troop.

With all the ingenuity of old campaigners, the soldiers soon had a fire lit and their coats drying, while the youngest was sent in search of something to fill the cooking pot, which had not been used since leaving Scotland. When the general gloom had deepened and became night, the clothes were dry and most of the occupants of the barn asleep. Anstey had been provided with a corner and a bed of sweet-smelling hay, but despite her tiredness she found that she could not sleep, and lay awake, aware of the noises around her made by the sleeping men and the dozing horses, while the rain drummed softly on the tiles overhead. At last she fell asleep, only to waken near morning and realize that the rain had stopped and that the first adventuresome bird was singing.

Unable to stay where she was, Anstey scrambled silently to her feet and picking her way cautiously over sleeping figures, crept softly to the huge double doors. Struggling to open them quietly, she slipped through the crack into a bright new world, made fresh and clean by the rain and the new day. Gathering up her long skirts, she crossed the wet grass to a nearby clump of trees, and leaning against a rough trunk looked out at the sparkling countryside. Round about more birds joined in greeting the morning. Gradually the sky lightened, the horizon becoming pink until the colours spread and faded into blue as the sun rose.

A movement beside her made Anstey turn her head to find that the Captain was leaning against a neighbouring tree watching her. Seeing she was aware of him, he prised himself away from the trunk and came towards her. "I had not known you were a lover of nature, Miss Frazer," he said.

"You should see our Scottish dawns – from a mountain you can really see the morning break."

He seemed not to be listening to her, leaning his hands either side of her head and staring down at her. Perplexed, Anstey frowned, and looked up to find his face disconcertingly near. Slowly he leaned forward, bending closer until his mouth was only inches away from hers.

"Captain Ward – are you ill?" she asked, and then his mouth touched hers, gently at first, his lips soft and caressing and then with a murmur he caught her roughly to him, crushing her against his chest as his kiss became more demanding. Hardly aware of what she did, carried along by fierce emotions that surprised her, Anstey slid her arms around his neck and returned his kiss.

Suddenly his grip slackened and at the same time she became aware that his skin was unnaturally warm. Drawing back she tried to look into his face, but his head fell forward and he slid slowly to his knees. Supporting him as best she could, Anstey called loudly for aid.

The door of the barn burst open and dishevelled, bleary-eyed soldiers appeared, struggling with clothes and hastily caught up weapons.

Sergeant Wright quickly took in the scene. "Fever," he said after a brief examination and ordered two troopers to carry their officer back into the barn.

"What shall we do?"

The soldier sucked his teeth reflectively. "No doubt there's a village close by – I'll ride there and see where we can find lodgings and a doctor, while you, miss, look after the Captain. You're a sensible female and I know there's no need for me to tell you how." He smiled briefly and touched her arm. "Don't look so worried, miss, Captain Ward is as strong as a horse, he won't die yetawhile!"

Anstey's eyebrows rose at his reassurance and she hastily disclaimed all anxiety on the Captain's behalf, yet wondered a little at the knot of apprehension that had formed in the pit of her stomach.

Going back into the barn as the Sergeant rode off, she made sure that the fire was kept up and the Captain placed close by on a pile of dry straw. Lacking any form of medicine, all she could do was sit beside his restless form and bathe his burning forehead with a handkerchief dipped in a dish of cold water. Under her worried eyes James Ward seemed to grow worse by the minute and Sergeant Wright to have been gone for an age, when in reality less than an hour elapsed before his return.

"The doctor's away – but there's a woman who'll give him a room. She says she can treat him with herbs."

He paused expectantly, but Anstey, more used to herbal remedies in her distant home than a doctor who was only sent for when all else had failed, was not disturbed.

"Have you brought a cart for him to lie in?" she asked, and stepped aside at his nod to allow the limp form of the Captain to be carried to the waiting farm wagon.

One quick glance at the neat house and its owner told her that she need have no qualms about the soldier's care or comfort, and feeling she had found an ally, Anstey smiled down from the cart into the woman's brown, wrinkled face.

Her hand was taken in a firm, comforting grasp, but the other gave all her attention to the sick man, examining him briefly before allowing him to be lifted out of the straw cocoon Anstey had arranged about him and carried to the waiting bedroom.

Sergeant Wright pulled off the heavy black jackboots and eased away the smart scarlet coat. Captain Ward groaned, and when his shirt was removed and Anstey saw the red, swollen wound high on his shoulder she could not suppress a gasp of dismay which contrasted oddly with the indifference she had assumed.

Will Wright shrugged. "I've seen worse. When it's cleaned up it won't look so bad."

The old woman leaned over her patient and clicked her tongue impatiently. "Why you men can't look after yourselves I'll never know. Too used to your mothers caring for you, I suppose."

Her voice was educated and the Scots girl opened her eyes a little, for she had supposed her to be a common country woman, but now she saw that while her dress was old, it was of good material and that the lace on her cap was of cobweb fineness.

Satisfied with her examination, she stood back and nodded to the girl. "He'll do," she announced. "The wound is inflamed as you can see, and he's in a fever, due no doubt to getting wet, but he's young and healthy and will mend quickly. Now, be off,

Sergeant, and see to your men. They can camp in my outbuildings but I'll not have any flirting with my maids . . . and you, miss, can stay here and help look after your young man."

Anstey felt some explanation was owed and attempted to make known the situation, but the older woman brushed aside her stumbling phrases, saying kindly that first they would see to the comfort of the patient.

"I'm Betty Coke," she said, "but most people call me 'Dame'. At my age one isn't used to answering to one's first name."

One of the maids entered with a can of hot water and the soldier's wound was cleaned and bandaged, a cooling drink of herb tea was spooned between his lips and Anstey persuaded to take a rest and refreshment in another room.

"Luce will sit with him and call if we are needed," she was told soothingly as Dame Coke led her away. "The fever will break tonight unless I'm mistaken, but you have nothing to fear. He will do better with me than with a doctor who would bleed him and make the poor man weaker."

"In Scotland we have our wise women who are relied upon for most things," Anstey said, realizing that the older woman assumed her to be worried on the soldier's behalf and unable for some reason to disillusion her.

"The women in my family have always been wise in the use of herbs and plants. The knowledge was handed on from mother to daughter. I have no children, so my knowledge will die with me, unless I can find the time to finish the book of simples I am writing."

Anstey found the scratching of her quill strangely soothing as, later, she sipped her shallow dish of China tea while the Dame took the opportunity to continue her self-imposed task. Not until that moment had she realized how she missed the gentle atmosphere of a home and the presence of a friendly female companion.

As expected, the Captain's fever broke that evening and he fell into a deep, peaceful sleep which lasted well into the next day. Anstey, who had been given the task of sitting beside him and calling as soon as he awoke that he might be given nourishment as soon as possible, occupied the time in mending the bullet hole in his shirt.

Looking up from her work, she found her eyes dwelling on his unconscious face, which seemed strangely young and defenceless without his usual straight grey gaze. Without his white wig she saw that his own hair was almost black, cut close to his head, not shaven as were most gentlemen of fashion.

Anstey sighed and returned to her stitching, smiling a little that she should be darning Captain Ward's shirt when a short while previously she had been prepared to kill her Redcoat captor. Involuntarily she glanced again at the bed and found herself the object of its inhabitant's gaze.

"So domestic," he murmured and she was surprised at the weakness in his voice, but when she leaned closer she could read the amusement in his eyes and knew that he had been struck by the incongruity of her task as she had.

"Dame Coke set me to it," she declared, hastily depositing the shirt on the seat of her vacated chair.

"Now you are awake, I'll go and ask for nourishment for you."

Before she could leave, fingers closed over her hand and she was held token prisoner.

"Not before you have answered my questions — where am I? I've vague recollections of being shot . . . but what then, and where the devil is my troop?"

Anstey looked down at him, aware that his touch was sending a pleasant tingle down her spine. To counteract her feelings, she answered with more asperity than necessary.

"You had a fever, which was your own fault for you would allow no one to tend your wound and insisted upon riding through a storm. As to where you are?" She shrugged, "I can only tell you that you lie in Dame Batty Coke's second best bed."

The Englishman regarded her silently, one black eyebrow crooked. "You've forgotten my soldiers," he reminded her.

"About the countryside. The Dame has taken the opportunity of using their strength and expertise to mend various gates and fences that have long lain in wait for a man's ability."

He roused himself in bed. "She sounds a formidable female. I take it that it is she I have to thank for this," he indicated the neat bandage across his chest. "If you would retire, Miss Frazer, I shall dress and present my thanks to her in person."

For all his brave words it was the next day before he left his room, but once up he regained his strength with surprising speed and soon declared that they must be on their way.

"To deliver that sweet creature into the hands of a

brutal goaler," put in Dame Betty roundly, having heard Anstey's story and making no effort to hide her feelings upon the matter.

"That sweet creature, as you call her, put a pistol ball into an English officer, killing him," Captain Ward told her, nettled.

Dame Betty snorted derisively. "If you believe that, you're more of a fool than I take you for," she retorted.

James Ward left his comfortable chair abruptly and strode to the window. Staring out of the room, he said harshly, "She has confessed."

"She's shielding someone."

He swung back into the room. "Pre-cisely," he agreed. "Who would carry your wager?"

Dame Betty looked up from her writing. "I think you know," she said quietly. Their eyes held for a few seconds before she nodded slightly, and a smile passed between them.

They left Dame Betty's house the next day, Anstey finding herself strangely reluctant to leave the shelter and unquestioning acceptance she had found there. The thought of London less than sixty miles away and the fate she would find there, loomed large in her thoughts, making her nervous and tense. Somehow the very solidarity and cosiness of the countryside through which she was riding seemed to present a danger, and she turned with passionate longing to thoughts of her wild homeland.

Trying to recall every curve and boulder-strewn slope of the mountainsides she had known since childhood, she rode with her head sunk upon her chest and oblivious to her surroundings until, sensing some unease among her companions, she lifted her eyes and looked around.

The road they were following had just breasted a hill and ahead, silhouetted against the sky, was a tall post that carried a swaying, creaking burden. Puzzled, she examined it, frowning as she tried to make out what it could be. Suddenly James Ward barked the order for men to close ranks round her, but not before she had realized with sickening clarity that she was looking at a gibbet and its ghastly load. Even as the soldiers pressed closely about her, she caught sight of a strip of material hanging from the corpse, its bright red and green faded and pathetic, but still recognisable as tartan.

"Dear God!" she exclaimed and bent over her pommel, one hand to her mouth as she fought the waves of sickness that threatened to overwhelm her.

Her bridle was taken and the soldiers increased their speed, as eager as she to leave the gruesome spot behind. Scarcely able to keep her seat, Anstey slumped in the saddle, while shuddering which she was unable to control shook her. At last their speed slowed and as they drew to a halt, brandy was forced between her pallid lips.

"That – was a man," she whispered, choking on the spirit. "*That* was my countryman."

"I would that you had been spared the sight."

Suddenly she lifted her head to stare at the Englishman her eyes wide and fearful. "Will – they do that to me?" she asked.

"No."

For a moment longer she held his gaze and then turned away with a choked sob, the reality of what she faced in London brought clearly home to her as it had never been before. Subdued and quiet, they rode on, even the soldiers uneasy when they contemplated what the fate might be of the prisoner they had guarded for so long. For the first time since leaving Scotland thoughts of escape filled Anstey's mind with ceaseless activity. Wild, impossible schemes chased each other through her brain and she wished bitterly that she had taken the chance offered her when Caroline's plan had been sprung earlier.

Even while she planned and rejected, she still had sense enough to present a dejected, despondent air that left none of her watchers in any doubt of the hopeless despair that held her in thrall.

As she had hoped, the soldiers displayed their consideration and tact by leaving her alone and when the column halted for a rest, she was able to delay her dismounting until she was the only one left on horseback. Waiting until the troopers had withdrawn from her somewhat, their attention taken up by the prospect of a few minutes' relaxation, she suddenly clapped her heels into her mount's sides and was several yards away before anyone realized her intention.

Unable to choose her moment for escape, she had been forced to take the one presented to her and had hoped that once round the curve ahead she would find some means of eluding her captors. The hoped-for woods or valleys failed to materialise, and instead she found herself faced by a long open road with not one atom of cover or even a side turning until it reached a bridge over a broad river a mile or so distant. Realising that she must either give up or trust in her horse's speed and stamina, Anstey hesitated momentarily, before a picture of the gibbet's grim burden flashed through her mind and without thinking more she kicked her heel against her mount's side and urged him forward.

Crouched low over his brown neck, she gripped the pommel with her knees and thought longingly of her despised breeches and the ease of riding astride. The wind snatched at her elegant hat and tossed it away, dragging her hair free of its pins and ribbon to fly behind her like a shining banner. Heedless of her own safety, she plunged on, exhorting the horse to even greater effort. She was sure that pursuit was close behind, but could spare no energy to glance over her shoulder, controlling the great beast under her was taking all her strength and skill, and she knew that one moment's lack of concentration could cost her dear.

The bridge seemed to fly towards her with frightening speed and she could see that the water was white beneath it with the turmoil of a weir that fed the mill on the further bank. A voice behind her, much nearer than she expected, called upon her to halt, but torn between exhilaration and terror, she galloped on until a hand grasped her bridle and brought her to an inexorable stop on the very edge of the stone bridge.

The horse plunged and trembled beneath her, shaking his head nervously while flecks of foam covered his smooth neck. Shaken by her struggle for breath, Anstey glared at her captor.

"Am I never to be rid of you?" she gasped. "You are like Nemesis—"

"Once in London—"

Her eyes opened wider at mention of the town which to her brought only fear and the thought of an ignominious death. With an inarticulate cry of repugnance and refusal she jumped down from her saddle, and despite her shaking knees dashed across the bridge and scrambled up on to the parapet.

"Anstey!" cried the Redcoat as he divined her purpose and leaping from his own horse, ran towards her.

Ignoring his shout, Anstey gathered up her trailing skirts and ran along the narrow stone edge, the swirling water beaten to a foam by the force with which it fell, dazzling her until she was giddy and deafened. Fearful, yet fascinated, she hesitated until the soldier's hand touched her skirt, and then with a cry of despair she leaped forward into space.

The roaring water seemed to rush towards her but suddenly something stopped her fall with a jerk and she hung suspended by the length of her full riding skirt that James Ward had caught in a desperate grip. Spray wet her hair as she dangled with her head lower than her feet, while above her anxious voices called and heavy boots thudded over the bridge. At last, after what seemed like an age, she was hauled upwards and dragged over the parapet by eager hands, to stare at her rescuers with wide, blank eyes that were dark hollows in her white face.

Shocked, the troopers stared back, shaken by the unexpectedness of her action. Quiet and uneasy, they formed a circle round her. White and shaken himself, Captain Ward glowered down at her, holding her elbow tightly as though expecting her to make another attempt to escape.

"You little fool," he snarled, shaking her, "you might have been killed."

"I wish I had," she flared, to cover her own fright.

Not sure herself whether she had sought death in the weir, or had only jumped in the desperate hope of escape from the impossible situation in which she found herself, she hid her feelings in a show of temper. "You saw that thing on the gibbet – do you think I want that to happen to me? I'd rather take my chance in the water. At least I might escape from you savage barbarians. The natives of America are more civilized than you."

"We don't roast our enemies over a fire—"

"No – you hang their bodies alongside the road and leave them to rot or be pecked by carrion, and you call yourselves civilized!" She looked round at the encircling Redcoats and made a derisive noise through her nose. "Look at yourselves. A whole troop to take one woman to London. Do we Scots affright you so?"

"You are overwrought," James Ward's face was tight with anger, but he made an effort to speak in a conciliatory tone.

"Anyone would be, having been confronted by your cruelties," Anstey cried, wishing she could throw herself into the Redcoat's arms.

"I am sorry you saw—"

"I'm sorry for the man whose body it was."

"In any country there must be law and order. He was a rebel."

"One cannot rebel against a usurper—"

"King George is King of Scotland. Accept it, Anstey Frazer, there is nothing you can do about it. You cannot defeat us all by yourself."

Anstey brushed away furious tears and hid her face against the rough stones of the bridge as one painful sob escaped her.

"Now, miss," Sergeant Wright patted her shoulder. "Don't take on so. Things'll come right, you'll see. No harm'll come to a nice young lady like yourself. Take my word for it."

"I wish I could," Anstey sighed and gave him a weak smile as she allowed him to lead her to where the horses patiently cropped grass.

For the moment she was exhausted by the strong emotions that had burned in her, now she could do no more than sit her horse and long for the end of the journey, whatever it might bring. Her long hair blew about her face as she rode, but uncaring of her appearance, she made no attempt to tidy it.

Subdued by the near-tragedy, the soldiers rode close about her, their attitude protective rather than that of goalers, but the girl sat in their midst aware only of one thing, that London was steadily growing closer.

She shivered at the thought and stole a glance at the English officer, longing for a gesture from him that would show that he still felt some kindness for her. In the wake of the wild emotions that had recently filled her came a void that had gradually been replaced by a reluctant acknowledgement of the fact that, with the perversity of nature, she had grown to love her captor; some time during the last weeks her hate and dislike had turned to something far different, and now she wished only to conceal her self-realization from James Ward.

Riding on with averted eyes, she knew that one kind word, one softened gesture from the man beside her would be her undoing, but Captain Ward looked steadily ahead, apparently oblivious to her presence.

CHAPTER
NINE

Now the way was quick and easy. The Great North Road was wide and well made, and with each mile seemed to grow busier and more crowded. Coaches and wagons passed in quick succession, strident trumpets declaring their right to the road as they hurried by the troop. Curious faces peered at Anstey from the depths of luxurious carriages, making her lift her chin higher as she pointedly ignored them. Several times the huge, lumbering stage-coaches lurched by, their horses stretched to a gallop as the drivers concentrated on keeping a good speed. The outside passengers hung over the protecting rails in their eagerness to see Anstey, so obviously a prisoner guarded by the column of soldiers.

Anstey's one thought now was to arrive in London without her feelings for Captain Ward being revealed. Aware of his nearness with every nerve in her body, she took refuge in silence, hoping that it would be accepted as a natural reaction to the fate that awaited her. By careful manoeuvring she managed to avoid the Englishman; without seeming to ignore him, she accepted others' aid in mounting or another's hands to lift her from the saddle, taking care never to be in a position for a private word or look.

But all her efforts came to nothing for Captain

Ward, well aware of her attempts, simply took the procedure of sending for her one evening with a firmness that brooked no refusal on her part.

The inn in which they were lodging was old, its rooms low and panelled. As she followed the red coat of her escort down the stairs and along the wide passages, Anstey toyed with the thought of the many other people who had walked the same boards on which she trod and, to keep her mind from the interview ahead, pondered upon their stories and the reasons behind their age old journeys, sighing to think of the lovers now dead and their bodies dust.

Captain Ward looked up at her entrance, his face curiously immobile and still as he indicated a settle facing the open window.

Anstey hesitated and made a tentative bid to avoid what she sensed would be a painful confrontation. "I really am very tired—" she began.

"I am well aware that I have driven you to the point of exhaustion and believe me, I would not disturb you, save that we need to talk upon a matter of the utmost importance."

He took a few restless steps about the room, turning before he reached the window to stop and look down at the girl, his face in shadow and his expression unfathomable. Staring down at her hands clasped in her lap, Anstey waited wondering what he was about to say, but instead of speaking, Captain Ward thrust his hands deep into his breeches pockets and gazed out of the window at the people passing in the street below.

Raising her eyes cautiously, Anstey studied him and knew by the set of his shoulders that his recently-healed wound was paining him. Even as she watched, he put up a hand and rubbed it absent-mindedly. The silence grew, and the girl began to wonder if the Redcoat had forgotten her presence. Captain Ward turned abruptly and took a breath as though about to speak, but seemed to have difficulty in finding words.

"Some time ago I offered you my friendship," he said at last, speaking quickly and without his usual assurance. "Which you refused – as you had every right to do if you wished. However, I feel that the circumstances have changed somewhat and that now you realize that you stand in need of a friend. It would not take a sharp imagination to dread the future and to be afraid of what is to come when you reach London."

Wondering where this conversation might be leading, Anstey tried to read his expression, searching his face for some clue, but with the window behind him, he remained a baffling silhouette.

"I would not bring to your mind something which I am aware you would prefer not to think about, save that we will reach London tomorrow—"

Involuntarily Anstey gave a gasp of dismay that she was unable to conceal, and felt her heart begin to race under the tight lacing of her stays.

"I have been given a set route to follow, and handbills have been handed out to the populace with details of your charge." He waited for the meaning of his words to dawn on her, but as her face remained blank and puzzled, went on to explain. "Which means that crowds will gather to watch us ride through the city to the Tower."

"Oh, no!" she gasped, understanding at last.

"I am afraid it will be – unpleasant." He continued quickly as Anstey closed her eyes and leaned back in her chair, one hand hiding her mouth. "There *is* one way to avoid such a happening."

Slowly the girl opened her eyes and looked at him · with mute appeal, her face pale with dread.

"As my wife, you would be protected from such an ordeal."

Her eyes widened as she stared at him, wondering if she could have heard rightly. For a second he held her gaze, reading her astonishment with wry amusement before seating himself beside her; then he added to her surprise by taking one of her hands in a warm grasp and advising her kindly not to worry.

"Wife!" she could only repeat weakly.

"As my wife you would not be expected to ride through London to provide entertainment for the mob, and I am sure that if you were married to an Englishman who could guarantee your good conduct in future, a whole new complexion would be put on your trial."

Anstey had not been listening. "But – are you saying you love me?" she cried and held her breath while she waited for his reply.

He had stiffened at her words and she sensed his withdrawal although he still retained her hand.

"I had not supposed that love came into the matter," he told her, and reading his expression, Anstey knew he was remembering the many times she had proclaimed her hate for him.

"I was proposing a marriage of convenience," he went on.

For a wild moment the Scottish girl had thought

that he returned her love, and now turned away to hide her bitter disappointment as she realized that he had only offered her marriage out of sympathy for the plight in which she found herself.

"If the matter went as far as a trial, which I doubt, you would certainly be acquitted. As mistress of Wrexford Manor you would be a lady of some substance and with my mother and sister there, not lacking in company. I would expect you to give me an heir, of course, but apart from that my demands would be few as my army duties would often take me away."

"Why?" she asked. Although knowing the answer, she had to be certain of his reason. "Why do you offer me marriage, Captain Ward?"

The grey eyes fell under her questioning gaze, and he examined her small hand which he still held. "During our time together, I have come to admire your courage and strength of spirit," he told her quietly. She was silent and after a short pause he continued.

"For all your protestations, I am certain that you did not shoot Leo Smythe but are protecting a member of your family . . . and, in some measure, I feel involved in your ordeal. Having brought you away from your homeland and subjected you to the hardships of a long journey without regard for your comfort or sex, my conscience tells me to make what amends I can."

Anstey sighed and gently removed her hand from his grasp. "It seems a very poor reason for marriage," she said reflectively.

"Do you expect me to declare my undying love?" the man beside her queried.

Lifting her head, she studied his face. To her ears

his question held a jeering note and her own expression settled into one of pride and indifference.

"No!" she said forcibly, to hide her feelings. "I would find it of the utmost embarrassment."

"At all costs we must avoid embarrassing you," Captain Ward agreed between his teeth. A moment ago he had found himself on the verge of declaring his affection, but wary of the Scottish girl's reaction and unwilling to be humbled, he had restrained the impulse, and now was certain that her dislike of himself was as strong as ever.

Sitting very straight, he folded his arms and stared at a point above Anstey's head. "You still have not replied to my proposal," he pointed out icily.

"I am aware of the honour you do me," she began, recalling her manners, but was interrupted by a snort of impatience from the Captain.

"Yes or no, Miss Frazer?" was his ostensibly weary question.

"If I marry, Captain Ward, which seems very unlikely in view of the future, it would be for mutual love and respect, not to ease a guilty conscience or to avoid an unpleasant happening." Her eyes were bright with tears as she faced him. "But I do thank you for your offer . . . I am aware of the effort it must have cost you to make it, and I assure you that there is no need for you to feel constrained to offer your name to me. You have always been fair in your attitude towards me, while I . . . have perhaps taken advantage of my sex to annoy and plague you. I am well aware that if I had been a man, my treatment would have been much harsher."

She smiled tremulously and stood up, shaking out

her velvet skirt. "And now, if you will allow me, I should like to retire."

James Ward's expression had softened during her speech and he made an involuntary gesture towards her, but, her eyes blinded by tears that she refused to let fall, Anstey did not see his proffered hand. Eager to leave the room before her distress became uncontrollable she turned, brushing aside his unseen arm, and ran from the room leaving the English officer alone with his own troubled thoughts.

Once in her room, Anstey flung herself face down on her bed and gave way to her emotions, stifling her sobs with her handkerchief. At last, drained and exhausted, she fell asleep, to wake abruptly to a dark room and the night air stirring the window curtains. Rising, she poured water into the basin on the washstand and rinsed her face and hands, before going to stare out of the open window at the silent sleeping world beyond.

Resting her hot forehead against the cool panes of glass, she idly looked down at the yard below, her attention suddenly caught by a still figure among the shadows. While she watched he moved slightly, the moonlight striking his white wig, and she recognised the tall figure of the English officer. Deep in thought, he smoked a long clay pipe, his head sunk against his chest.

Drawing back into the safety of the shadows, Anstey gazed down at the soldier, aching with a wild longing to go to him and accept his offer of a few hours previously, even while she knew that the action would be foolish and one that she would regret. Once or twice during their long journey she had thought his manner towards her had softened, but she knew now that it had only been his natural gallantry to a female in an unhappy situation. Knowing herself only too well, she was perfectly aware that she could never be satisfied with anything less than love in her marriage, she could never be happy, even wed to the man she loved, if the only feelings he had towards her were those of guilt and duty.

At last the man below stirred. Pushing his shoulders away from the wall, he looked up at her window, the moon etching the planes of his face in black and white. Involuntarily, Anstey backed hastily into the shadows behind her, and as though he had seen the movement and recognised her, Captain Ward lifted his hand in what might have been a salute. His arm fell to his side when she did not reply and pausing only to give a slight nod in her direction, he turned and marched briskly away, the metallic jingle of his spurs carrying clearly across the silent night.

A sleepless night had done little to quiet Anstey's fears of meeting the London mob and she rose nervous and apprehensive, unwilling to face the new day. Some perversity in her nature made her take especial pains with her appearance, pride making her present her best impression to the hostile world.

The English officer was waiting for her at the bottom of the stairs and came forward as she appeared.

"I would spare you this," he said quietly, "but if I refused the duty, another would take my place and he might not be inclined to have a care for you."

"I understand," Anstey responded, pulling on her gloves and settling the wide sweep of her riding skirt more gracefully over her arm. Taking pity on Captain Ward's obvious worry, she told him kindly that she had no intention of throwing a fit of the vapours.

"I have no fear of that," he assured her, "but rather of what you might meet during the day."

Anstey could think of nothing to say, having faced the memory of the crowd at Grantham during the long hours of the night. "I'm ready," she said evenly and accepted his arm.

Sliding her fingers into the crook of his elbow, she was comforted by the warmth from contact with a fellow human and allowed herself to be led out into the road where the troopers were already mounted and drawn up in two rows.

"We'll look after you, miss," whispered Sergeant Wright as he helped her to mount. "The Captain ordered that all our pistols and muskets should be loaded, so you've nothing to fear."

Anstey shivered a little at what the Captain's fore-thought implied and seeing her expression Will Wright hurried to reassure her.

"Not, of course, that we expect to use them, but it's best to be prepared, like. So never you fear. You may be a Scot and a rebel, but there isn't one of us as wouldn't defend you."

She could only smile tremulously and thank him quickly before the order to move off was given and the double column trotted smartly between the rows of houses.

The troop of soldiers drew only cursory glances from the walkers they passed and Anstey could only conclude that the handbills had not penetrated so far out of the city. Soon, however, the people began to thicken, at first only a few waiting on the village greens as the column approached, but by the time they arrived at Islington, the crowd was two or three deep. A few shouted and some small boys threw stones, but the Scots girl felt that her worst fears were groundless until the villages were left behind. As the houses became closer together, so the people grew steadily thicker until, by the time they entered the City Road, crowds of jeering, gesticulating humanity were lining the road.

The soldiers closed about her, Captain Ward placing himself at her side, doing his best to shield her from the missiles which suddenly showered about them. A stone struck a horse, making him start and rear, while the troopers kept their faces carefully blank as rotting vegetables and refuse fell among them. Grateful for the Captain's protecting bulk, Anstey lowered her head against the flying filth, trying not to see the excitement on the faces nearest to her.

Suddenly something white flew through the air and landed among the folds of her habit. About to brush it off, Anstey stopped in amazement, almost unable to believe her eyes, as she stared down at a white rose lying on her lap. Incredulously she picked it up and smelled it. As the heady perfume filled her nostrils, she glanced across at the man by her side. Holding his grey eyes with hers, she raised her chin and defiantly tucked the rose into her buttonhole. Frowning, he reached out and would have snatched the blossom away, but even as his hand touched the soft petals a voice rose about the murmur of the mob.

"That's right, my pretty – show 'im you're not afraid," advised a crone raucously. "Law love you, I 'ates to think what you've 'ad to put up with alone with all them soldiers all the way from Scotland!''

Those nearest her laughed and the sally had to be explained to others who had not heard. Suddenly the mood of the throng changed; the Londoners' usual dislike of authority returned, and the fickle crowd was ready to take Anstey to its heart. To her astonishment her progress down Bishopsgate and along Eastcheap was almost a triumphant march. Flowers were tossed towards her and smiling she gathered them up, and by the time they reached the Tower of London, had quite a posy.

Suddenly a shadow fell over her as they rode under an arch and the girl shivered at the unexpected chill. A gate closed behind them, shutting out the crowd, and Anstey looked about with startled eyes, realizing for the first time that they had arrived at their destination. The posy fell from her nerveless fingers to be trampled unheeded under the hooves of the soldiers' horses, while fright, like a physical pain, closed tight fingers about her heart.

Grey stone walls and black arrow-slits seemed to dance madly round and round and she closed her eyes against a deadly giddiness which seized her. James Ward was just in time to spring forward and catch her in his arms as she slumped in the saddle.

Sick and trembling, Anstey fought against the faintness which threatened to overwhelm her. She could not explain the flood of fear and apprehension that the grim fortress had engendered in her, knowing only that the ancient walls and cold stones had so filled her with despair and foreboding that she had come near to losing consciousness.

The Redcoat's strong arm held her steadily and for one moment she allowed her head to rest against his shoulder. Under her ear she could hear the regular beat of his heart and was seized by a wild longing to stay in that position for ever, safe from the dreaded future that awaited her. Instead she opened her eyes and found Captain Ward's gaze upon her face, with such an expression in his own eyes that for a second she could not speak.

Immediately his eyes were shuttered and careful blankness settled over his face, leaving Anstey to wonder if she could have been mistaken in thinking that for one second she had read love in the gaze bent upon her.

"P-pray put me down," she managed to say and at once she was set upon her feet, the Captain keeping a supporting arm about her waist.

An elegantly-dressed gentleman came forward and made a bow as he introduced himself. "I am the Governor of the Tower. Until recently I have had the honour of looking after three of your fellow countrymen."

Anstey was unable to repress a shudder, knowing he was referring to the three Scottish peers who had been beheaded a few weeks previously.

"My Chief Warder will take you to your cell. Perhaps we shall meet later for dinner, when I shall look forward to hearing your adventures. I assure you I have no prejudice against the Scots – in fact I only parted from your peers with the greatest regrets."

Anstey looked at him with horror, until she realized that far from attempting to terrorize her, the Governor was making what he considered to be small talk. Instinctively she leaned nearer to the Redcoat.

"Miss Frazer is feeling a little unwell," put in James Ward quickly, making her grateful for his intervention. "With your permission I will accompany her to her . . . accommodation."

"Just so – I quite understand. The journey must have been a trial . . . for all concerned. I've put her in the White Tower, a little unusual, but then we've not had the care of a lady rebel before. My Warder will escort you." He gestured to a stout man in the uniform of a Beefeater to show them the way and with another elegant bow sauntered away across the Tower Green towards his own house.

Perhaps when it had been new the White Tower had lived up to its name, but now its walls were only a little lighter in colour than the others that surrounded it. Crossing the expanse of grass towards the building, Anstey was surprised to notice a quantity of large black birds hopping about, eyeing her with disconcertingly human interest.

"Ravens!" she ejaculated, having no difficulty in recognising them, but somewhat surprised to encounter them in such surroundings.

"The legends say that England will fall when the ravens leave the Tower – so their wings are clipped," Captain Ward told her laconically.

They had reached the entrance to the tower by this time, and Anstey could think of nothing to say as she gazed at the immense building which seemed to hang over her with a grimly menacing air to its ancient fabric. Pausing on the step, she turned to look back at the courtyard behind her and saw the troopers who had escorted her for so many miles, sitting their horses like statues. At their head, Sergeant Wright raised his hand and saluted gravely. Acknowledging his gesture, the girl took a last look round before, yielding to the pressure of Captain Ward's hand on her arm, she crossed the threshold and the heavy door thudded closed with a finality which made her heart leap against her ribs.

The passage in which she found herself was extremely dim, being lit only by a single narrow slit window on the stairs ahead. Aware of her nervous fears, Captain Ward tightened his hold on her elbow reassuringly.

"You'll get used to it in a minute," he said. "Close your eyes until you are accustomed to the darkness."

"Not afraid of the dark, are you, miss?" asked the warder, climbing the stairs and shutting off the meagre light with his bulk as he passed the tiny aperture.

"I – don't like small places," Anstey confessed, following him.

"Then it's a good thing the Governor thought to put you where he did. Some of the cells aren't fit for a pig, let along a lady like you. *Your* cell is like a little palace, with a window and all. My wife's to look after you, so you'll live like a queen while you're with us."

He laughed at his joke and, wheezing slightly, opened a door and stood aside for the girl to enter.

Slowly Anstey walked into the room, strangely reluctant to look about her. When at last she raised her eyes she found she was in a small square cell, its walls of grey stone scratched here and there with initials or devices, its only window set deep in the thick wall above her head, through which could be seen a patch of sky. A table and chair and bed were its only furnishings.

At once her situation was brought forcibly home to her, and she was seized by an uncontrollable urge to escape. Panic-stricken, she turned back, conscious only of a wild desire to break out of the building that was to hold her prisoner, and found herself against James Ward's red-clad chest.

Her hands held captive against his scarlet coat, he recognized the signs of rising hysteria in her wide eyes and white face, and changing his grasp to her shoulders shook her slightly.

Slowly Anstey relaxed, the wild look leaving her face as her breathing returned to normal. Across the room the warder's eyes met his and obeying the jerk of the soldier's head towards the door, the older man nodded amiably and ambled out.

Once alone, the soldier produced a purse which he dropped into Anstey's hand, closing her fingers over it when she instinctively protested against the gift.

"Take it," he commanded. "The warder seems a good enough fellow, but you'll find you have need of money."

He seemed to have forgotten that he still held her hand, and finding the contact singularly comforting, Anstey allowed her fingers to lie in his grasp and said nothing except her thanks for his gift.

Drawing her to the other side of the cell, Captain Ward put himself between her and the open door and bent towards her ear. "I had meant to say nothing in case it came to nought," he whispered for her alone to hear, "but seeing you so despairing and afraid, I feel I must urge you not to give up hope that all will yet be well."

Anstey searched his face with her eyes, but when she drew a breath and would have questioned him, he laid a finger over her lips and shook his head.

"I can say no more – save that it would make me happy to know that you considered me your friend."

Not stopping to think of the incongruity of such a request in the circumstances, Anstey assured him that she did. Forgetting that they had been captor and prisoner, she impulsively gave him her other hand. "Shall we meet again?" she asked, unaware of the wistful note in her voice.

"I give you my word," the Englishman answered, lifting her hand to his lips.

For a moment his grey gaze held hers and then he was gone. Anstey looked after him blankly as the door was closed and locked, and then almost involuntarily she raised her hand and pressed the back of it to her mouth.

CHAPTER
TEN

SOMEWHAT to her surprise Anstey found confinement in the Tower of London not so irksome as she had imagined. The Warder's wife, Mistress Potts, proved a cheerful motherly person, who by producing a few homely touches, soon managed to give the cell a more comfortable appearance. While nothing could alleviate her claustrophobic dislike of small places, the Scots girl found that her jail was made bearable by the fact that she was allowed to walk on the ramparts each day and even sit on the Tower Green under the careful eye of a guard.

From the ramparts she could see the River Thames, broad and deep, with a myriad of varied craft on its shining waters. She could never cease to be amazed at the diversity of the small boats plying their trade and larger ships arriving from foreign parts that filled the river with life and interest. Sometimes she could even catch the exotic smell of spices as a ship returned laden with expensive luxuries from far-off places.

Not long after her arrival she was joined on the green by the Governor, who dismissed Mrs. Potts with a nod and seated himself beside her on the stone bench.

"Not finding your stay with us too tiresome, I hope?" he asked, taking snuff from an elegant box, and went on without waiting for an answer. "However, I am sure that you will be – interested – to know that your trial has been set for two days' time."

While she had expected the news every day, now that it had come Anstey was shocked into silence, her heart beating like an imprisoned bird against the bones of her bodice. "W-where?" she heard herself ask, in a voice totally unlike her usual tones.

"Westminster Hall – the seats and scaffolding have not yet been removed—"

The Governor broke off abruptly, sending her an uneasy glance as he realized that he had been about to mention the Scottish peers who had recently been sentenced to death at their trial. "Baron Hardwicke will hear your plea," he finished weakly.

Anstey recognized the name. "Is not he the man who sentenced the three Scottish lords?" she asked, disdaining subterfuge.

"I am afraid he has no liking for the Stuarts or their cause," admitted the Governor. "In your case, I am sure he will sympathize with your youth and sex and be lenient."

Privately Anstey doubted it, but her natural pride made her assume a brave front, and when later the Governor left her, she hurried to look over her meagre wardrobe and decide upon the most suitable dress to wear. She was sighing over the choice between the clothes Molly Barton had chosen for her all the time ago when she had lodged in the Sour Plum, and the riding-habit belonging to Caroline Ward which now was sadly worn and travel-stained, when the Warden's wife appeared in the doorway.

"This was sent for you, miss," she said, proffering

the large bundle she carried. When the Scots girl looked questioningly at her, she went on, "Came this morning, it did. 'Cause my man had to open it in case something was hid in it. Someone's sent you some clothes to wear, ducks."

Dropping the bundle on the bed, she soon produced a blue velvet bodice and a full tartan skirt which she shook out and held against her ample form.

With a lift of her heart which was almost painful Anstey recognized the bright colours of her own tartan. "Highland dress!" she cried joyfully. "Who could have sent me such a thing?"

"Don't know, I'm sure," commented Mrs. Potts, "but it's very pretty, I must say." She watched as the other seized it and held the soft wool against her cheek, her hands caressing the familiar pattern. "There's been talk of banning it, so I've heard."

Anstey looked up, her hands suddenly still. "Banning it?" she repeated in a puzzled voice. "*Banning* tartan?" Her voice rose as the full implications struck her. "We'd never accept it – we'd lose our identity . . . how could they enforce it? There are some clansmen who never come down from their clachans in the mountains."

She stroked the soft material with a loving hand and smoothed the velvet of the bodice, pausing as a new thought filled her head. "Will they let me wear it?" she asked.

"The Governor said he had no objection, so I don't see why not," said Mrs. Potts. "They can hardly drag it off you in Westminster Hall. You wear it, my pretty, and show us Londoners what a Scottish lady looks like."

Following her advice and the dictates of her own heart, Anstey dressed next morning in the costume she had not worn for so long, revelling in the familiar sight of the neat bodice clasping her waist and the gay check billowing above her ankles. Almost carefree, she took particular trouble over arranging her hair, pleased to find that it had grown enough to allow her to twist it on top of her head in the style which she knew was most becoming. By association, her thoughts turned to the Redcoat officer who had cropped her hair, and she wondered if he would have charge of the soldiers who would escort her to her place of trial.

When, a short while later, she was taken out to the coach that would carry her through London, Captain Ward's familiar figure was nowhere to be seen and Anstey felt an irrational dismay at his absence. None of the impersonal troopers were familiar to her, their blank gazes passing over her head with disinterest as she climbed into the heavy black coach.

To her surprise she found it already occupied and, dazzled by the change from sunlight to dark interior, started back in alarm until she heard the Governor's reassuring voice.

"I am to accompany you," he said, his eyes scrutinizing her dress with approval. "May I compliment you on your costume? Like most of my fellow-countrymen, I find such simplicity vastly becoming."

Anstey smiled her thanks. "Do you know who sent it?" she asked quietly.

The Governor shook his head. "Whoever it was had good taste – and sense," he commented. "I have no doubt that it will create a good impression. You should be grateful to your benefactor, whoever he is."

"Is it true that tartan is to be banned?" Anstey could not forbear asking.

"There is talk of it – and of breaking the old clan system. Justice and punishment would no longer be in the hands of the Lairds, but by appointed officials."

Anstey was horrified. "The clan is a family," she protested. "Our chieftan is regarded as a father."

"Justice should be impartial – your method can be nothing less than personal. Likes and dislikes, animosity and remembered happenings must come into it, and pervert the course of justice. What if a clan has a bad or corrupt chief at its head?"

Remembering Sir Robert Mackenzie, the girl fell silent as she recalled his past iniquities and the many whispered complaints of his unfair jurisdiction and biased judgements in favour of his toadies and friends.

"But all chiefs and lairds are not like that," was all she could say, as much to herself as to her companion.

The elegantly suited shoulders opposite lifted and fell expressively. "There is good and bad in all things," he said, and leaving her to her own thoughts, fell to gazing out of the window at the passing streets.

The coach and its escort seemed to make little impact upon the people thronging the narrow streets. Busy about their own affairs, they scarcely spared the sombre vehicle a passing glance, in contrast to the crowds who had watched the Scots girl's progress through the capital on the day of her arrival.

Relieved not to be the butt of their interest, Anstey hoped that she would be spared the ordeal of a noisy, excited audience at her trial, but when she was escorted into the splendour of the ancient hall, built by William Rufus not long after the Norman Conquest, she was met by a sea of expectant faces, peering down at her from the tiers erected for the trial of the three Scottish peers a few weeks previously.

Stumbling involuntarily as she was greeted by a loud, indistinct murmur of anticipation, Anstey was grateful for the Governor's reassuring presence as he escorted her to the high box-like structure intended to place her in clear view of all the observers.

When she had recovered her equilibrium enough to raise her head and gaze out at the sea of faces turned in her direction, she surreptitiously searched for a bright red coat and a familiar face, hoping to see the upright figure of James Ward among the crowds of strange and unfriendly people. Sighing inwardly at his absence, she turned her attention to the men and women seated on the tiers, wondering why they should have chosen to spend their time watching a Jacobite on trial, if not necessarily for her life, certainly for her liberty.

All kinds were there and all stations in life, from painted drabs and respectable working-class matrons, to lords and ladies in their shimmering silks and satins, who held nosegays to their aristocratic nostrils against the smell of the common folk who crowded so uncomfortably close to their betters' well-bred sides.

A ripple of anticipation moved the audience like a wind across a field of corn and following their eyes, Anstey saw a stern, middle-aged man in a full-bottomed wig appear as the people rose to their feet. Accompanied by a retinue of solemn attendants, he made his way slowly towards the high chair on a dais in the middle of one wall and Anstey realized with a sinking of her heart that this hard featured man was Philip Yorke, First Earl of Hardwicke, an implacable enemy to the Stuarts and their followers, who had so recently, and in the same hall, sentenced three of her countrymen to death for their part in the Jacobite Rising.

Across the empty space between them their eyes met, and the Scots girl shivered involuntarily under the icy stare that studied her briefly but astutely. In that short glance, Anstey felt her innermost soul had been laid bare, examined fully and put aside for future consideration.

Clutching the rail in front of her, she fought back a wave of fear as she realized instinctively that she could expect no mercy or clemency from the man sent by the Hanoverian King to judge her. Studying the grave, implacable face now turned from her, she knew that cold justice according to the law of the land would be allotted her and nothing more.

A black-clad figure knocked a gavel on a table and the crowded hall grew silent, leaning forward in their seats, watching the prisoner with excited anticipation.

Anstey stared back impassively, her face schooled to careful blankness, her chin lifted unconsciously as she faced her accusers with all the pride and arrogance inherited from her Highland ancestors.

The trial began. As a prisoner of state being tried for treason she was allowed no advocate, and had to listen in silence while a long accusation was read aloud. The people on the tiers gasped and muttered angrily as they heard of the death of Leo Smythe, and Anstey shivered under the concerted gaze of their hostile eyes.

The drawling voice droned on, the lawyer's affected accent strange and hard to understand to Anstey's ears. Before long her attention wandered and she found herself following the progress of a bee that had wandered by chance into the hall, with more interest than the lawyer's monologue could arouse. She knew that she would be allowed to speak when all the evidence had been given but until then she had to listen in silence and unable to sustain interest in the familiar story, she fell to improving the speech upon Scottish loyalty she had prepared during the long days of her incarceration in the Tower.

Suddenly an awareness of a change in the proceedings caught her attention and she looked up quickly, realizing that the prosecuting lawyer had returned to his seat and that an anticipatory silence hung over the ancient hall and its inhabitants.

Lord Hardwicke shuffled the papers in front of him, his hands sure and methodical as he replaced them in the exact centre of the table. At last he looked up, his cold gaze passing over Anstey without a sign of interest, before he gazed out over the sea of absorbed faces staring back at him.

"Before we proceed further," he began in a dry, precise voice, "I understand that one of His Majesty's officers has something relevant to say. This event is most unusual, I may say, but as the King himself has given permission for this evidence to be heard, I can only order it to be given. Is Captain Ward here?"

Startled, Anstey lifted her head abruptly to look eagerly around the assembly. A movement in the far corner caught her eye and her heart gave an excited skip as a tall figure in familiar regimentals marched forward. She recognized the sturdy figure of Sergeant Wright keeping step at his elbow and could not repress a feeling of relief at the Redcoat's unexpected arrival.

James Ward appeared pale under his pristine white wig and black tricorne, but the irrepressible Sergeant gave her a wink as he passed. Across the width of the hall, Captain Ward caught her eye and sent her a message so full of meaning that her heart lurched and then began a violent tattoo against her ribs.

"You are Captain James Ward of His Majesty's army, and also of Wrexford Manor in Lincolnshire?"

"I am."

James's clear voice echoed about the blackened beams, and the audience stirred in anticipation, agog at this unexpected event.

"I understand that you have His Majesty's permission to place before us some new evidence appertaining to the trial of Miss Anstey Frazer?"

"I have."

"Then proceed."

Pausing deliberately, the English soldier turned and sent the girl in the dock a reassuring smile, before he positioned himself so that he could be seen by both the judge and lawyers and the watchful spectators.

"My lord, may I crave your indulgence? If you will allow me a few minutes to explain the situation I will then give you a letter from France which will, I feel, put a new light upon the matter before you."

Lord Hardwicke waved an elegant hand and taking it for permission, the soldier continued, his even voice carrying clearly to the furthest corner of the hall.

"I was assigned the duty of escorting Miss Frazer from

the Keep of Cushlan in Ross-shire to London, where she would be put on trial for the murder of Captain Smythe. Leo Smythe was a friend of mine, which made the duty onerous in the extreme. As you may guess I knew a ready dislike of Miss Frazer even before I met her. Ready to believe the worst of her, I both despised and detested her, treating her without regard to the respect her sex and position demanded. I assure you, my lord, I was not – kind, during the difficult and dangerous journey through Scotland."

Under the concerted, speculative gazes turned on her, Anstey felt heat burn in her cheeks and hastily looked down at her hands clasped tight on the rail before her.

"However, eventually Miss Frazer's demeanour was such that even I began to wonder if the accusation could be true. She made no effort to hide her loyalty to the Pretender, but here I felt she was following her father's politics, as all good daughters should, rather than her own inclinations. As I grew to know her, under the most trying of circumstances, I became more and more certain that the hand that pistolled Captain Smythe was not that of Anstey Frazer, even though she insisted that she alone had killed him. In fact at one point in our journey she was the means of saving my life. If not she – then who? Her sister Isabel, a lady of beauty but known to be simple, seemed unlikely. After much thought I grew interested in her young brother, Jamie—"

"James! No, please!"

Anstey's voice cut across his words with a wild force that shattered the calm that held the audience enthralled in the soldier's narration.

Crossing the floor to her box, Captain Ward reached up and covered her hand with his, ignoring the interested eyes watching. "Have no fear," he told her. "Trust me. All will be well, you have my word for it."

He gazed deeply into her eyes, before returning to his former position and resuming his story. As she followed his tall, straight figure with her eyes, without thinking her hand smoothed the fine wool of her tartan skirt. Suddenly her fingers grew still and she gazed down at the gay checks, speculation rushing through her brain. When she lifted her head she had no doubt at all about the identity of the person who had sent the parcel containing the Highland dress she was wearing.

"Upon being questioned closely about this matter," James went on, "Miss Frazer always denied that anyone else was involved, seeking to divert my interest to her own guilt by various methods at each mention of her brother. With this in mind I recalled that Jamie Frazer had been hiding in the Scottish mountains, but upon enquiry found that he was known to have escaped to France, where he had joined his father in Paris. I therefore took furlough from my regiment and set out for the French capital, determined to seek the truth. I found the Frazers living among the Jacobite refugees, and once they had learned my errand was received kindly by them. Master Jamie freely admitted that his was the hand that fired the fatal shot. Coming in from a day's hunting he had found Isabel apparently struggling in the arms of an English officer, and only afterwards discovered that the man had not been molesting her, but seemed to be under the momentary impression that she was his wife. Indeed, having seen portraits of the two ladies, I can vouch for the fact that they closely resemble each other. I must add that Captain Smythe's wife had lately died and that the undoubted shock of encountering Isabel Frazer, so like her, must have resulted in behaviour which affrighted the lady, whom you will remember was a simple, child-like person."

The people in the seats sighed and murmured, bending towards each other as they exchanged views upon the story. Waiting until they had settled again and had turned expectant faces towards him, James Ward continued his tale, with his audience hanging upon his words.

"Jamie Frazer wrote a letter confessing the crime, and expressing his sorrow for causing another man's death." Taking a folded, sealed paper from his pocket, he handed it up to Lord Hardwicke. "He makes it clear that Anstey Frazer came upon the scene of the tragedy and taking charge, sent her sister to the care of their former nurse and, afraid for her brother's life, sent him into hiding until a boat could be found to take him to France. Anyone who dearly loves a young brother can easily understand why she took the guilt of murder upon her own shoulders."

He paused and looked round before taking another letter from his pocket, and even Lord Hardwicke appeared interested as it was presented to him.

"Upon my return from France I presented myself at Court, where the King was kind enough to see me and to listen to my story. He gave me leave to present Miss Frazer's tale here before you, my lord, and also charged me to give you that letter which would make

His Majesty's wishes upon the matter known to you."

An expectant silence fell as Lord Hardwicke's long fingers broke the royal seal and spread the thick paper out before him. It seemed to take an interminable time for him to read the few lines of writing that crossed it, but at last he looked up and raised his eyebrows.

"Do you know what is written here?" he asked.

"Not exactly," replied the soldier, "but – I have an idea."

Lord Hardwicke pursed his thin lips. "Then pray take a seat while I sum up," he commanded.

With another reassuring glance at Anstey, Captain Ward and his Sergeant left the floor and seated themselves on the bench that an usher indicated.

With all the skill of an actor, Lord Hardwicke waited until the excitement rose to a fever pitch and then quelled the restless crowd with a single cold glance.

"The prisoner will rise," shouted a black-clad usher, taking his cue with the ease of long practice.

With a start Anstey realized that he meant her and scrambled hastily to her feet, her eyes wide and fearful as she understood that the moment which would decide her fate had arrived. Impassively the judge stared back, and try how she would the Scots girl could discern no kindness or sympathy in his cool gaze.

"Anstey Frazer, you were brought here to stand trial for murder . . . and upon the evidence presented I find that under that particular charge there is nothing to be answered."

Anstey's heart gave a joyous bound as she took in

his words; however, her relief quickly abated as Lord Hardwicke went on, raising his voice above the murmur from the crowded tiers lining the hall.

"However, it appears that you hold freely expressed rebellious views, and that your loyalty is openly given to the house of Stuart. You, madam, are a rebel and a Jacobite and must be confined until you learn different ways and new loyalties."

Afraid of what he was about to say, Anstey looked away, wondering desperately if she was to be sent to the Tower for life or shipped to the Colonies as a bonded servant.

"I must confess that my judgment would be harsh — I have no sympathy with treachery or treason, but with true generosity His Majesty is prepared to be lenient, and having taken into consideration your youth and sex and obvious loyalty to your family, he believes that in time you may become a true subject. With this in mind he orders me to release you into the care of a good and loyal Englishman — with the proviso that within three days you marry the said man."

Speechless, Anstey gazed across the hall at him, almost unable to believe what she had heard, while the murmur from the excited crowd grew into a thunderous roar that filled her ears and made her head ring.

Raising his voice, Lord Hardwicke tried to make himself heard, but gave up and made an impatient gesture that the prisoner should be brought to his desk. Dazed and trembling, still unable to believe his words, Anstey stood before him while the mob behind buzzed like an angry beehive. Suddenly she realized that a familiar scarlet uniform was beside her, and felt her hand taken in a firm, reassuring grip.

"I have your word, Captain Ward, that you agree to this condition?" Lord Hardwicke's tone made his own opinion clear and he made no attempt to hide his disgust when the soldier nodded.

"Arrangements are already made," he said firmly.

The judge turned his cold gaze on the girl. "You, I may say, have no choice in the matter," he told her with some satisfaction. "Refuse the Captain and *I* have choice of a husband for you!"

Anstey lifted her chin. "I have every wish to marry Captain Ward," she told him, and felt the clasp on her hand tighten.

Lord Hardwicke dismissed them impatiently. "Then take her and make a good Hanoverian of her," he said and waved them away.

Almost before the watching people were aware of their going, they were whisked to a door and hurried along a passage which led to the back of the ancient building. Here Sergeant Wright waited with a coach and horses.

"Quick," he commanded, his eyes on the corner of the narrow street, "I can hear them a-coming."

Anstey was bundled without ceremony into the coach, James Ward climbed in after her, the steps were folded and the door slammed shut, just as the first of the crowd rounded the corner and gave a triumphant shout as he saw them.

"Off you go, sir," cried the Sergeant, and stepping back gave a smart salute as the horses bounded forward.

Anstey found herself suddenly tongue-tied. Confused and embarrassed, she was unable to even look at her companion.

"W-what a handsome equipage," she said at last, her voice totally unlike her usual tones.

"Will Wright hired it for me." By his voice the Captain too, was having difficulty with his vocal cords. He cleared his throat and began again.

"Quite different to the one—"

"Not at all like—"

Breaking off, they stared across the narrow interior at each other, Anstey waited, her face in shadow, hoping that at last the English soldier would show his love for her. Instead he stirred slightly, avoiding her eyes, and turned his head to gaze out at the passing streets.

As the constraint grew between them Anstey stared down at her hands clasped in her lap, desperately trying to think of something to say that would ease the tension.

"I – must thank you for your part in my release," she ventured at last, unhappily aware that her gratitude sounded cool and grudging.

"No need," James replied, his tones matching hers. "I am only sorry that you are being forced into a match which must be distasteful to you."

To his listener, he seemed to imply that he found it so himself and Anstey grew still, her heart sinking at his words as she realized that any kindness towards her on his part must have been merely imagined or simply the normal attitude of a gentleman. As for his part in her release! His journey to Paris and the final outcome due to his efforts on her behalf must be due solely to his desire for the truth, and an honourable solution to an affair in which he found himself inextricably involved.

"Pray order the coach to turn about," she said, suddenly resolved upon the only course of action that presented itself to her. "I find this marriage unacceptable."

For a long while James Ward stared across the confined space at her, his expression inscrutable, then, "Be damned if you do, madam," he drawled slowly and stretching out his long legs, leaned back and crossed his arms. "By the King's orders you must take a bridegroom—" he went on, but Anstey broke across his voice.

"I am well aware of that," she declared impatiently, "and will take my chance with Lord Hardwicke's choice."

"Now, there you are quite wrong," Captain Ward told her, his drawl much in evidence. "An you marry anyone it will be me – think you that I am willing to be made a laughing-stock? The trial will be reported in the papers and the outcome popular knowledge. I'll take you for my bride, Miss Anstey Frazer, whether you will or no."

By now Anstey found the idea that she had ever wanted to marry the infuriating Englishman quite ludicrous. "Sassenach," she snarled, her eyebrows together in a scowl.

"Call me what you will in that heathen tongue of yours – it will not make one iota of difference." He studied his nails before allowing his indifferent gaze to travel slowly over her. "I had an idea that you might jib at the last moment, and with that in mind I took the precaution of arranging for a member of the clergy to be awaiting us at Islington."

Aware of her struggle to find words to express her

feelings, he allowed himself to smile into Anstey's furious eyes. "We'll stay the night at the inn there. The landlord's a rogue and will care nothing if the ceremony is performed tonight . . . or in the morning."

Watching her face, he was satisfied that she had taken in his meaning and giving a slight nod, he settled back against the padded seat and appeared to go to sleep.

CHAPTER
ELEVEN

ALTHOUGH she had passed through the village of Islington on her way to London, Anstey found that she had no recollection of it beyond remembering a group of people on the green who had been the first of many to stare at her that day when she had ridden to the Tower.

Looking out of the window as the coach stopped she saw that the inn was built in the black-and-white style to which she had grown accustomed as she had travelled the length of England. Its low windows twinkled in a friendly manner and the stout landlord stood bowing in the wide entrance, a smile of welcome on his glowing red face.

Thinking to throw herself on his mercy, she put out a hand to open the door, only to have her wrist taken in a strong grasp as James Ward reached across her to turn the latch. His hands seemed to linger as, not waiting to lower the steps, he lifted her to the ground. Almost at once her wrist was imprisoned again and he turned to command dinner and a room for the night.

"Landlord," Anstey spoke loudly, her voice clear and firm, "I am being abducted. This man is keeping me a prisoner against my will."

The landlord's small eyes studied her before he turned enquiringly to the Redcoat. Reaching into his pocket, Captain Ward slipped something that chinked into the readily outstretched hand, and at once the man was all ingratiating smiles.

"The lady grows maidenly," James told him. "We must pander to her desire to appear reluctant – I do assure you that a moment ago she was all eagerness. I have need of your best dinner and chamber to overcome her modesty – and privacy, if you please."

The men exchanged meaningful glances and the soldier jingled the coins in his pocket invitingly "And in the morning – if we have enjoyed our stay – you shall be well rewarded."

Bowing so low that his nose almost touched his knee, the landlord assured him that he, personally, would see that they were as private as the grave, and ushered them into the inn. Aware of the knowing glances of the servants Anstey schooled her features into indifference and ignoring the ill-concealed grins directed towards her, allowed herself to be led into the inn, which seemed suddenly to have lost all signs of welcome, appearing instead to her jaundiced eyes to be shoddy and badly managed.

The room into which they were shown would, under any other circumstances, have presented a comfortable, cheery appearance, but now the velvet curtains seemed tawdry and cheap, while the heavy furniture was oppressive and old-fashioned. Chairs and a gate-legged table waited by the open window for a meal to be served on its polished surface, while a massive four-poster bed seemed to dominate the room with its presence.

As soon as a small chest was brought in and stood on a table by the bed, James dismissed the servants, turning to Anstey impatiently as soon as they were alone.

"Well?" he demanded. "I mean us to be wed – whether before or after is up to you. The Reverend Mr. Ford will call this evening when his duties allow. You have until then to make up your mind."

Anstey eyed him, "La," she said, apeing the accents of the English ladies she had heard, "I vow that I had no idea that you were so mad with desire."

James Ward's mouth twitched and he took a quick step forward. "The main desire I feel, madam," he said dangerously, "is to wring your neck."

"No wonder Englishmen haven't a name as lovers!"

"Later, ma'am, we shall prove the truth of that."

His grey eyes held more than a hint of a threat and Anstey quailed under his menacing gaze, needing all her resolution to hide the growing fear she felt. At first she had believed that he had no intention of carrying out his threat, but with every passing moment she became more convinced that James Ward was determined to wed her – whether she was a willing bride or not.

Since the joy of learning her sentence from Lord Hardwicke earlier that day, everything had gone wrong. She had thought by his attitude that Captain Ward shared her happiness at the order that they should marry, by his acts of kindness had supposed that he cared for her; but now there seemed to be only enmity and anger between them. With one last attempt at the happiness that seemed to be eluding them, she turned impulsively to him, her voice and manner soft.

"James," she said, almost pleadingly, her hands out

to him in a supplicating gesture. After a perfunctory knock the door behind him opened, attracting his attention as she spoke, and he did not hear her gentle voice, or see her pleading gesture.

"Dinner, Captain," announced the landlord. "Oysters, as you ordered, to put the lady in a better mood, followed by roast duck and a dish of my wife's syllabub to follow. You'll find it a meal fit for a King, if you will allow me to say so."

Quickly the table was set, and ushering the servants before him, the landlord bowed himself obsequiously out of the room.

"Come to the table, Anstey," the soldier commanded quietly, and Anstey, who had kept her back to the room with great determination whilst the table was laid, turned reluctantly. "You have not eaten since this morning – come and break your fast."

She was suddenly aware of a gnawing hunger awakened by the succulent odours from under the silver covers, and her legs seemed to convey her, of their own accord, across the room. The Redcoat held the chair for her, bowing with a flourish as she seated herself, his hand brushing her shoulder as if by chance, but with a lingering touch that made her as aware of his fingers as if they had burned her.

As though unaware of the sensation he had aroused in her, Captain Ward took his place opposite her, pouring wine into the tall glasses.

"Oysters?" he enquired blandly, proffering the dish of large grey shells.

"No!" Anstey, who had heard of the delicacies before but never seen them, shook her head violently, aware of the landlord's remark as she did so.

"Ah, well, each to his own taste," murmured the soldier, tossing several of the fish down his throat with evident enjoyment. "Let me help you to some duck," he said a little later, proceeding to carve the golden bird and fill her plate.

Carefully ignoring the watchful eyes of the man opposite, Anstey kept her eyes on her plate and ate her fill, making the meal last as long as was possible. Slowly spooning the cool froth of the syllabub into her mouth, she grew uneasy under the gaze of his heavy-lidded eyes, feeling her breath quicken and her hand begin to tremble until at last she dropped the spoon into her dish and felt impelled to raise her eyes to meet his.

Leaning back in his chair in an indolent manner, he was sipping from a tall glass, grey eyes half-hidden beneath black lashes. Deliberately allowing her to read his gaze, he smiled and raised his glass in a salute before drinking as he held her glance with his.

"To us," he said, letting his look wander over her in a manner which made Anstey blush and look hastily away.

To hide her growing agitation, she reached for her glass and took an unwary gulp of wine, choking slightly in her haste and uneasily aware that the soldier had left his seat and come round the table. Careful not to turn her head and without raising her eyes, she could see his white breeches and the skirt of his scarlet coat as he stood beside her. She raised the glass again with an assumption of ease she was far from feeling, and to her chagrin her hand shook so much that wine slopped on to the table. Strong brown hands removed the glass from her grasp and then Captain Ward took firm hold of her shoulders and lifted her to her feet.

At his touch Anstey's resolution broke; she had meant to be calm and persuade him by her quiet eloquence into letting her go, to turn him from his determination to take an unwilling bride merely as a sop to his pride, by her show of common sense which would brook no argument. Instead of which, she found herself turning in his grasp and reaching almost involuntarily for his face with her nails.

Her hands were seized and twisted behind her back, but not before she had left angry red marks down the brown cheek. White with fury, he jerked her against him and held her tightly, not caring that he hurt her. Twisting his fingers in her hair he pulled her head back.

For a second she had a confused impression of ice-cold eyes glittering down at her, before his mouth closed over hers. The kiss lasted a long time and had nothing of love in it; speaking rather of rage and frustration and the age-old desire to conquer that men felt towards any female who dared to display wills of their own.

Half-dragged off her feet as he held her against him, Anstey lay in his arms, staring up into his face, while tears of anger and fright hung from her lashes. "I hate you!" she declared passionately.

James Ward laughed and held her closer. "Before the night is out you'll love me," he promised, and bent his head over hers again.

Knuckles knocked discreetly at the door behind them. "The Reverend gentleman is here, your honour," called the landlord's voice.

Slowly the Redcoat lifted his mouth from her

bruised lips. "Well, Anstey?" he asked slowly. "Which is it to be?"

For a moment she searched his implacable face, seeking for some softening, some sign of slackening in his resolution. Seeing no tenderness in his cold eyes, she sighed and looked down at the gold frogging on his scarlet coat.

"I – would leifer far be wed at your home," she ventured, hopeful of winning a few days' respite during which anything might happen.

The soldier shook his head and called over his shoulder to the landlord. "Pray ask Mr. Ford to call back tomorrow—"

"No!" In her agitation she plucked at his buttons, pulling and twisting at his jacket with nervous fingers.

He waited with eyebrows raised. "What, then?"

"Please, James . . ." Sensing the implacability in his still figure, she faltered into silence. "Very well," she went on after some minutes during which he waited, unmoved by her inward struggle against capitulation. "I will marry you tonight, but first you must allow me time to attend to my toilet," she added hastily, still eager to win a reprieve, however slight.

"My dear," he said softly against her hair, "I have known you too long to be taken in by such soft words. As soon as I left the room you would be climbing out of the window. No, Anstey, we will be wed at once – if that is your wish, of course."

She looked up at him, her eyes bright with frustration. "You know full well that the last thing I wish for is you as a husband!"

"As soon as our nursery is full, you may go your own way," he promised, releasing her abruptly, only to take a grip on her arm above the elbow and urge her towards the door, calling to the waiting innkeeper to retain the obliging clergyman a little longer as he did so.

The Reverend Mr. Ford awaited them in the parlour; a tall, thin man in the dark garb and white bands of a village clergyman. Turning to Anstey, he bowed with a singularly sweet smile which was at once saintly and absent.

"I am James Ward of Wrexford Manor in Lincoln-shire, and this is my bride-to-be, Mistress Anstey Frazer," announced the soldier.

The clergyman took Anstey's hand. "We meet upon a joyous occasion," he said, happily.

As she took a deep breath preparatory to making her situation known to the Reverend Mr. Ford, Captain Ward's fingers bit warningly into her upper arm and, considering the consequences to herself should she refuse a wedding, Anstey remained silent, railing inwardly against the perfidy of the man beside her.

". . . where can we find a bridesmaid?" asked the clergyman, who appeared totally unaware of the agitation that beset the bride-to-be. "And you, Captain Ward, have forgot to provide yourself with a best man."

"If I must have one, the landlord will serve," the soldier replied carelessly, "and I dare say his wife or a maid will support my bride."

At last all was arranged; the landlord's rosy daughter was called from her usual duties and the innkeeper himself removed his apron and, donning a snuff-coloured coat, professed himself ready and willing to act the part of friend to the bridegroom. Almost at the last minute, his daughter exclaimed and left the room suddenly, to reappear a short time later and thrust a bunch of hastily-gathered flowers into Anstey's hands.

Touching her hot cheek to the cool petals of the full-blown roses, Anstey thought that ever afterwards the heady perfume would remind her of her wedding day, recalling the sadness she felt as she stood beside the man whom she had foolishly imagined loved her.

Mr. Ford's voice droned on and she gave her responses automatically, scarcely needing the tightness of her captor's grip as the clergyman paused. At last the ceremony was over and a heavy gold signet ring encircled her finger, feeling strange and unfamiliar.

"You may kiss the bride," said the minister indulgently, closing his Bible.

The Redcoat's hands were on Anstey's shoulders, turning her to face him. A knuckle tipped up her chin and for a long moment James Ward stared into her eyes before bending his head. He kissed her gently, his lips lingering on hers.

As he turned from her to pay the clergyman and dispense largesse to the witnesses, Anstey's hand crept to her mouth, her eyes watching the tall uniformed figure with something like bewilderment in their depths; the caress she had just received had been totally unexpected. Since she had made up her mind to his dislike of herself, his action, which was almost tender, had taken her by surprise, filling her with disquiet and upsetting her carefully controlled emotions.

Unwilling to have her hopes dashed again, she

refused to consider the possibility that James Ward might feel affection for her, and resolutely turned her mind to means of frustrating his plans – not even to herself would she admit that in reality she only half-wanted to escape from the bridegroom forced upon her. Part of her longed for his touch and was excited by his presence, while her pride fought against such weakness, willing to barter any chance of happiness in exchange for freedom.

As though aware of her scrutiny, the Redcoat turned and met her gaze across the room. One mobile eyebrow rose, his grey eyes so full of meaning that she looked away in confusion, burying her nose in her bouquet in the hope that the action would calm her nerves.

Intent upon studying the voluptuous blooms in her hands, she did not see him join her, and yet the touch upon her shoulder was so familiar that she was aware of whose hand it was as if by some instinct.

"Come and thank the Reverend Mr. Ford for his services," was all he said, but his hand slid slowly down from her shoulder, making her heartbeat quicken with a mixture of fear and anticipation.

Moving quickly away from his touch before any should notice his gesture, she allowed herself to be led to the clergyman and said all that was right and proper.

"Remember – be loving and dutiful, my child," he advised sanctimoniously, unaware of the seething emotions his words aroused in their recipient. "Woman was made to obey, as man was wrought to command."

Glowering after his retreating back as he thankfully

retired to the sanctity of his nearby vicarage, Anstey was aware of the amusement in the man beside her.

"I hope you will take his advice to heart," commented Captain Ward, "for there speaks an eminently sensible man."

"Pshaw!" snorted Anstey, "Any woman would tell you that the man is a fool! The Reverend Ford inhabits Cloudcuckooland, and speaks his lines parrot-fashion. If men believe themselves our masters it's because we allow them to do so – as an indulgent nanny would a fractious child." Glaring up at him, she made a discovery and stopped short just as she was about to muster further arguments. "I believe you are provoking me," she said.

He made her a small bow. "I own it's more agreeable to have you berating my whole sex rather than being the sole object of your dislike."

His breath fanned her cheek as he bent his head to speak for her alone. His nearness sent a tingle of excitement, almost a thrill of anticipation, through her and something in his gaze told her that he was well aware of her reaction.

"Let's to our room," he breathed softly, as his arm slid round her, drawing her close as he shielded her from the rest of the room with his body and bent to kiss her, gently but with an undercurrent of passion that left her more shaken than his previous forceful caresses had done.

For a moment she melted against him, responding to the hinted emotion he had allowed her to glimpse, but, happening to glance up, she read the triumph at her capitulation in his eyes and at once her pride came to the fore. Releasing herself she turned away, saying coolly, her voice as indifferent as she could make it, "As you will, sir, but first I would be alone." The glance she spared him was cold. "As a gentleman of honour, you will allow me that."

His arms fell to his sides and he stepped back. "Don't think to escape me, Anstey, for you are mine now and I have a liking to hold that which I own."

Her gaze was withering with contempt. "You have a wife, Captain, not a slave," she reminded him, and turning on her heel would have left him with a flurry of her tartan skirts, save that he reached out and caught her wrist in a grip that crushed her bones and swung her round to look at him.

"You may have ten minutes," he said between his teeth," and then I shall join you."

With flaming cheeks, but with her head held high, Anstey crossed the room, accepting the facetious remarks and innuendoes offered by the company as graciously as she could. Climbing the stairs to her chamber, she dismissed the landlord's daughter who had accompanied her, and once alone in the dark room made dim by the growing dusk outside, closed the door and leaned against its stout panels, momentarily allowing the dejection she felt to show.

Straightening her shoulders with an obvious effort, she looked up with sudden resolution and, having examined the furniture, began to drag a heavy wooden chest over the polished floorboards to the door, and then wedged it firmly in position under the drawn bolt. A heavy chair took all her strength to lift but, hot and flushed with exertion, she pushed it in place on top of the chest. Eyeing the edifice, she was struck by the obvious realization that the structure was too flimsy to keep anyone out, especially so determined a man as the Redcoat captain and, hunting feverishly around, began to pile any moveable object on to the bare surfaces of the chest and chair.

In the midst of this wild activity she seized the little chest that had been brought in earlier from the coach and, about to toss it to join the growing pyramid, she paused, wondering what it contained. Overcome by curiosity, she put it on the floor and lifted the lid, to find herself confronted by a sea of tissue-paper.

Tentatively, she raised one corner and peered underneath before, impatient with herself, she pulled aside the whole sheet and stared in amazement at the folds of soft silk and delicate lace that met her eyes. Almost of their own accord her fingers pulled out peignoirs and nightdresses and nightcaps, all of the most luxurious material and beautiful sewing. Sinking back on her heels, she smoothed the thin silk, running her fingers over the rich, thick lace, her expression both bewildered and thoughtful as a frown wrinkled her brow.

The breeze stirred the curtains at the open window behind her, but she knelt on, deep in thought and speculation until, suddenly scooping up a flimsy garment, she held the cool folds to her burning cheek.

"Did you really think that a barricaded door would keep me out?" demanded a voice behind her and, dropping the garment with an inarticulate cry, Anstey half-turned to find James Ward in the act of climbing over the window sill. "Luckily there's ivy climbing over the wall – I'm only surprised that you didn't make use of it yourself."

Brushing leaves and dust from his bright uniform

he stood up, regarding her intently for a moment as he noticed the opened chest. "Well, Anstey?" he queried quietly at last.

"I – found these." Her hands fluttered over the expensive feminine wear.

"You were intended to."

"You bought them?"

"Yes."

"For – me?" Her head bowed lower over the exquisite silks, her voice so low that the watching man had difficulty hearing her words.

Captain Ward allowed his amusement to show. "Who else?" he wondered.

"Oh, *James*!" The name escaped her on a sigh and a sparkling teardrop fell on to the pastel folds on her lap.

At once he was beside her, taking both her hands to lift her to her feet regardless of the lingerie that slid to the floor as he did so. "Crying, Anstey?" he asked softly. "Because I chose to give you a gift?"

She hung her head and would not look at him. "Things have gone so w-wrong," she said dolefully.

"None that cannot be righted."

Lifting her head she gazed fully at him, a question in her eyes, and he went on, clasping her hands to his red coat and speaking earnestly. "I have need of an heir if my name is not to die out. Divorce is long and difficult, but if you really feel that you cannot give me a child, then I shall see my man of business about having our marriage annulled."

A tear escaped and slid down her cheek while she stared up at him wordlessly, and after a while he went on again.

"However, if you could bring yourself to live with

me as my wife, I shall do all in my power to make you happy."

Her lip quivered. "I don't want to be h-happy – I want to be l-*loved!*" she wailed, and tore her hands free to dash away the scalding tears that blinded her. "I am not an – an English aristocrat to be satisfied by a marriage of convenience. I want to be loved – and to love my husband."

Taking her face in both his hands, he bent to stare into her eyes. Satisfied by what he saw there, he sighed and slowly shook his head. "Anstey, Anstey," he said softly, "how foolish we've been."

Her gaze widened. "F-foolish?" she repeated, while a wild hope began to unfold in her breast.

"Foolish beyond measure . . . we have fought and quarrelled, said and done things neither of us meant, while all the time—"

"Yes," she put in urgently as he paused, searching for the right words.

"We were afraid to admit our own feelings, afraid that the other would not return them . . . that we made ourselves vulnerable if we said, 'I love you'."

Shyly reaching up, she laid a hand against his cheek. "How very silly, to be sure," she murmured, her eyes alight.

Taking her hand he turned his face against it before kissing the palm, his lips lingering in the warm hollow. The touch sent a thrill of excitement through her, quickening her breath and weakening her knees as she swayed towards him. Melting against his body, Anstey felt herself dissolve into his embrace, losing her identity as their lips met in a long caress that left them both breathless and shaken.

"I – thought you were marrying me out of pique, because your pride was hurt," she half-laughed, knowing now how foolish her assumption had been.

"I wanted to marry you because I loved you, but I was so angry that I could have wrung your neck. You have a way, Anstey, of driving me to a rage which I find almost uncontrollable at times."

His confession gave her pause. "Will we deal well together?" she wondered.

"Better than most," James Ward told her firmly. "Since meeting you, my love, I find that milk-and-water misses have grown insipid. I have a liking for stronger fare which I never suspected until you came into my life. Without you, Anstey, life would be intolerably dull."

"Life without you, James, would be unbearable," she returned simply, and, exultantly, he gathered her up in his arms, sweeping her off her feet to lay her back against the high-piled pillows of the four-poster bed.

Sinking into their softness, Anstey slipped her arms round his neck and drew his head down to hers, giving herself up to the abandon of his kisses with a growing passion of her own. Their kisses deepened until each was aware only of the other's need as their bodies clung hungrily together. Feeling his fingers at the laces of her velvet bodice, Anstey abandoned the last remnants of her reluctance in excitement at his touch, her bosom rising and falling with the fierce emotion she felt.

Brown fingers pushed aside the lace shift she wore, his hand sliding across her smooth white shoulder in a caress that made her sigh with pleasure, and at last his lips found the soft hollow between her breasts. The touch filled her with exquisite joy and with an inarticulate murmur, Anstey shivered in his grasp, delighting in the strength and masculinity of the hard body that enveloped hers.

Love and desire overwhelmed her, and their passion consumed them until a bursting blaze of rapture united them in shared delight. Gasping, Anstey twisted her fingers in her lover's hair and drew his head down to her breast, unwilling to let the joyful moment pass, while she whispered sweet nonsense and soft words of love in her ear.

Later, fulfilled and happy, she fell asleep with her head on his shoulder, to wake some time in the night. The candles had long since burned themselves away and, turning her head, she found her husband watching her by the light of the moon, which stole in at the open casement and filled the room with a silver glow.

"James," she murmured softly, putting out a hand to him. At once it was taken and held against his heart. The touch of his warm smooth skin sent a tingle of exquisite pleasure through her. "You won't regret marrying me?" she asked tentatively.

For answer he bent to kiss her, but reaching up she placed a hand against his lips and held him off while she spoke. "A Jacobite wife will hardly further your career."

"Then I'll retire and spend my life as a country squire, devoting myself to the care of my estate and to the business of filling my nursery. With such a lusty husband, Mistress Ward, you will have no time for politics."

He had taken her hand and was in the process of

nibbling each fingertip in turn. For a while Anstey watched with absorption, until she managed to drag her attention away long enough to ask a question of overwhelming importance to her.

"And you, James, what of you?"

"I, my love, shall have time for nothing save the care of my home and its inhabitants. We shall be that most unfashionable thing – a loving wedded pair, facing the future together whatever might be, and each year growing more contented and more in love."

And, filled with pleasure and happiness at his words, Anstey gave herself up to his loving, knowing that in her erstwhile enemy's arms she had found the love that she had longed for since time began.

Masquerade

The sweep of the past...the warmth of romance...the lure of faraway places.

Masquerade

All the suspense...all the intrigue and mystery...the excitement and adventure of an age long past. Other worlds and other times...set against a background of pure romance.

MASQUERADE historical romances are peopled with striking characters, whose desires and destinies will enthrall you for hours.

Don't miss this thrilling opportunity to experience, through the pages of these 3 FREE books, an exceptional new reading adventure.

Get all the latest books before they're sold out!

As a MASQUERADE subscriber you will receive, approximately every 6 weeks, THREE exciting new MASQUERADE novels, immediately after they come off the press.

So join now...don't miss a single title!

Cancel your subscription whenever you wish!

You don't have to buy any minimum number of books. Whenever you decide to stop your subscription just let us know and we'll cancel all further shipments.